W9-BUM-876

KING

· A PROPHECY NOVEL ·

ELLEN OH

HARPER TEEN
An Imprint of HarperCollins*Publishers*

To my husband and best friend, Sonny.
I couldn't have done it without you.

HarperTeen is an imprint of HarperCollins Publishers.

King

HarperCollins Children's Books, a division of HarperCollins Publishers,
195 Broadway, New York, NY 10007.
www.epicreads.com

Library of Congress Cataloging-in-Publication Data
Oh, Ellen.
King : a Prophecy novel / Ellen Oh. — First edition.
pages cm — (Prophecy ; 3)
Summary: "Girl warrior, demon slayer, and tiger spirit of the yellow eyes—Kira is ready for her final quest to save her cousin, the young boy destined to rule the Iron Realm as crown prince, and to uncover the third lost treasure while facing innumerable enemies in order to fulfill the famed prophecy"— Provided by publisher.
ISBN 978-0-06-209115-4 (hardback)
[1. Adventure and adventurers—Fiction. 2. Demonology—Fiction. 3. Prophecies—Fiction. 4. Soldiers—Fiction. 5. Kings, queens, rulers, etc.—Fiction. 6. Fantasy.] I. Title.
PZ7.O364Kin 2015 2014027405
[Fic]—dc23 CIP
AC

Typography by Carla Weise
15 16 17 18 19 PC/RRDH 10 9 8 7 6 5 4 3 2 1
❖
First Edition

SEVEN KINGDOMS
Mt. Baekdu
N. WAGAY
BAISHAN
WUNU
Secret River God Lair
Yalu River
JINAN
NUMA
HEKOU
WANDO
GURU
HUSHAN
SINI
UJU CITY
Taedong River
OAKCHO
EAST SEA
N
WONSAN
Dragon Springs Temple
Mt. Hwaak
Nine Dragons Waterfall
HANSONG
TONGEY
Northern Mountains
Imjin River
HANSONG CITY
Bukhan River
CHUNCHEON
Diamond Mountains
MINCHU
Han River
Namhan River
CATHAY
KUDARA
JINHAN
Naktong River
NOSONG
KUMSONG
KAYA
Kum River
MUJU
Mt. Jiri
Flower Hill Temple
GEUMGWAN
YELLOW SEA
WAGAY
DONGNAE
MULHAY
MODO ISLAND
JINDO ISLAND
Miraculous Sea Crossing
YAMATO
T'AMNA ISLAND

Kira sat staring at the waves lapping on the sandy shore. She hadn't moved since Taejo had been snatched by Fulang over two hours ago.

Behind her, her brothers and friends were busy trying to prepare for her new journey. They'd left her alone, knowing she needed time to think. She'd gone from anger to despair to anger again. She burned with it, a fiery volcano.

In her mind's eye, she could still see the blue dragon's great wings beating up a sandstorm as he lifted Taejo and Gom into the clouds and disappeared from view. She could still hear Taejo's screams and Gom's distressed cries.

It was all her fault. She should have killed the dragon in the shadow world when she'd had the chance. Why had compassion stayed her hand? If anything were to happen to Taejo, she would have broken her oath to her uncle and father. Kira closed her eyes in pain. She couldn't bear the thought.

This is not your fault. This is fate.

Kira's eyes flew open in surprise. It sounded like Brother Woojin's voice. But he was three thousand *li* away. It would take him weeks of traveling to reach them.

"*Sunim,* I'm so sorry." She spoke into the wind, as if it would carry her words north to him. "It was my job to protect the prince and I failed."

You must have faith, my child.

Kira didn't know if it was really him somehow communicating with her or if it was just her mind telling her what she wanted to hear.

She sighed. "Faith is nice, but not much help right now. What I need is a plan. But I don't know what to do."

Brother Woojin's voice was silent. Instead, she heard the dragon again.

"Musado, *if you want to see the princeling alive, then bring what you have stolen from me to Tiger's Nest Temple on Jindo Island. You have ten days.*"

Gritting her teeth, Kira had to fight the rage that rushed through her once again. So much of the anger was directed at herself for failing to recognize the meaning of her weird visions. It was all so clear now that it was too late. Now that she had to chase a blue dragon to an island that had already been invaded by the Yamato and seek a temple filled with cannibalistic monks who considered her their greatest enemy.

Her head hurt.

Someone came and knelt in the sand next to her. "Your brother sent me to tell you they are ready for you," Jaewon said.

Kira rose to her feet, feeling stiff and tired. The afternoon sun had shone down brightly on her head and she was feeling the effects. Silently, Jaewon passed her a water bag. With a grateful look, she drank, feeling the slight headache start to give way.

They climbed up the dunes and over to the command center. Inside the large open tent, Kyoung, Kwan, and several military leaders were conferring. Her brother Kwan should not have even been there. Badly clawed by Fulang, Kwan was in no state to be standing for very long. She was about to tell him to rest when he spotted her.

"Kira, this is madness!" Kwan exclaimed. "You of all people are the one Daimyo Tomodoshi wants. He will use everything in his power to capture or kill you. And Jindo Island is swarming with Yamato!"

Her eldest brother seemed to notice her immediate aggravation. He grabbed Kwan by the shoulders and pushed him onto a short stool.

"Actually, Admiral Yi has figured out an ingenious way to get her to the island," Kyoung said.

The admiral bowed and stared at Kira with piercing eyes under shaggy, graying eyebrows that even his helmet couldn't cover up.

"Kang Kira, we may be in luck. For this is approximately the right time of year for the miraculous land bridge to appear between the islands of Modo and Jindo," he said.

"Miraculous bridge? What is it?" Kira asked.

"It's a well-kept secret that only the islanders know about. It occurs two to three times a year in the spring and summer. A land bridge that lasts for about an hour forms between the islands of Modo and Jindo."

"Only an hour? What time of day does it occur?"

"That's one of the problems. In the last five years, the first of the pathways has formed progressively later in the day," he said. "Our navigator predicts that it will open in the next four days and will be at around sunset. But it is also the most dangerous time. When the tide returns, it comes in hard and fast and will sweep you deep into the ocean."

"If it's not dark enough, we also risk being seen on the road," Kira said.

"That's the other issue."

"How is this helpful, then?" Kira asked sharply. "There's a bridge that may or may not form, and if it does, it might be while it's still bright out, in which case we'll be visible to the Yamato patrols. And even if we cross it, we risk being drowned by the tide!"

"I know it sounds like madness," the admiral said.

"There may be no choice," Kyoung said. "The entire Jindo coastline is heavily patrolled by the Yamato."

"This is not going to work!" Kwan said.

In the ensuing quiet, the admiral stared at Kira, appraising her.

"To be honest, I'd rather you not go at all. Our intelligence informs us that you are the number one priority for the Yamato. They want you captured alive."

"This is nothing new," she responded.

"The daimyo needs you for some reason. He is more interested in you than the prince. Falling into his hands will mean disaster for all of us."

"I understand, but I have no choice. I must go after the prince," Kira said.

The admiral seemed to be carefully pondering his next words.

"I must ask you if this is the right thing to do," he said slowly. "If they get their hands on you, it might be more dangerous than losing the prince."

"Never say that!" Kira responded fiercely. "He is our future king!"

Kyoung pulled Kira aside and placed a comforting arm around her shoulders. She could see the blackened fingers of his left hand, the remnants of his encounter with the Demon Lord's cursed blade that killed their uncle. She was reminded again of how much they had lost and suffered since the start of the war.

Lowering his head, he spoke to her in a soft undertone. "Kira, he speaks the truth," Kyoung said. "There can be other kings but there is only one Musado."

Shaken by his words, Kira pulled away. She was reminded of Shaman Won from Jaewon's village. The shaman had claimed that Brother Woojin was using Kira only to protect the prince. He'd accused the monk of not respecting Kira and seeking to minimize her role in the prophecy.

"Even recognizing that the girl is the Dragon Musado, your mind seeks a more acceptable interpretation. That she is only part of the prophecy instead of the only one. She is only relevant to you as the prince's protector. But what you fail to recognize is that everything is irrelevant without her."

The shaman was right. This was something that she was as much at fault for doing as everyone else. It had been difficult for her to accept that she was the Dragon Musado, and when she did, she still downplayed her own importance. To Kira, Taejo was the prophecy. He was the one she had to protect. When she'd gone to the Diamond Mountains and found the first of the Dragon King's treasures, the tidal stone, the Heavenly Maidens had told her that Taejo was the future king. It was her job to ensure that he saw his future through. She swore to take care of Taejo. It was a promise she would never break.

"I understand why it is you feel this way," she said carefully. "I appreciate your feelings. But please respect mine. I made a vow to his father and ours to protect

Prince Taejo. I must go after him. I must save him."

"Then we will honor your oath and speak no more of this. We will do whatever is needed to help you," Kyoung assured her.

They returned to the group. "The matter is decided," he said. "She must go."

With a decisive nod, the admiral began the discussion again.

"I understand that my plan sounds crazy, but here is what I propose. We set sail for Modo tonight, on the evening tide. It usually takes a full day of travel, although the seas have been unpredictable of late. We will arrive from the east, which will keep us out of sight of Jindo. You'll be dropped off in a small craft as close as we can get to shore. We cannot drop anchor, as we would risk being seen if a Yamato ship should pass by. It will be late in the evening and low tide, so it should be relatively safe," he said. "Once you get to the island, you have two options. The first is to keep an eye out for the bridge and make a run for it. The second option is to row over to Jindo. But it would take too long by yourself."

"I'm going with her," Jaewon cut in.

The admiral eyed Jaewon with approval. "Well, with two of you, it should take only an hour, provided the seas are calm. But that leaves you sitting ducks for the Yamato if they spot you."

Kwan cursed. "That's an even worse option!"

Kira rubbed a finger along the scar that ran from her

eyebrow to her cheek. "We must pray to the Heavenly Father for a moonless night."

The admiral's expression turned crafty. "Well, here's the exciting part of my plan. We will create our own diversion." He pointed to the map of the southern tip of the peninsula. "Our navy has had great victories against the Yamato in the East Sea. We have pushed them west. But I have an idea that will send their naval forces a punishing blow."

He pointed to Jindo Island on the southwestern tip of the peninsula. "Modo Island is this tiny point right here to the east of Jindo Island. The channel between Jindo and the mainland is called the Roaring Channel because of the fierceness of its tides. It is the fastest of all our waters. This strait is treacherous, for it shifts directions from north to west and then back every three hours. We will draw the Yamato fleet into the Roaring Channel as the tides are changing. My sailors know how to navigate the channel, but the Yamato don't. If we time it right, they should incur tremendous damage without us even firing a shot at them."

"But how does that help my sister get to Jindo?" Kwan asked.

On a piece of parchment, the admiral used a fine paintbrush to highlight the area. "Here is the pathway. It leads to this shore point. The patrols cover several areas along the coastline. Four nights from now, you will wait on Modo for my signal." He then drew their attention to a small covelike area on the eastern side of Jindo. "We will engage all the Yamato on the north side of the island. At the same time we will attack this entire northeast coastline, drawing all the patrols away. When you see the night sky light up in flames that will be your signal. Only then should you run across the pathway, if it is there, or row your boat over to Jindo. Hopefully that will buy you enough time to cross over without being seen."

"We really need to know how long that path will stay open," Jaewon said, "and whether there will be time enough to cross it."

The admiral's craggy face was creased in concern. "While we think it is approximately an hour, we've noticed that the later in the month that the pathway forms, the shorter the time it stays open."

"Exactly how far is it?" Kira asked.

"Almost seven li," he said.

Kira smiled in relief. "That would only take us half an hour to run," she said.

"I have to warn you that its appearance is gradual. That's why you must be vigilant about watching for it. The hour starts as soon as it shows. You must plan accordingly."

Jaewon and Kira looked at each other uneasily.

"Admiral, if it is open less than an hour, and we have to wait until it is dark enough, there's a chance that we won't make it," Kira said.

"Or we wait until it is completely dark and row over," Jaewon said.

Kwan shook his head in frustration. "Rowing takes a

lot longer. More time for a patrol to come back and spot you. Neither of these options will work."

It was dangerous, relying on the fallibility of the Yamato patrols and the aggressiveness of the admiral's naval attack.

"I know it's risky but it's the best option available to us," Kira said.

Kira thanked the admiral. "It's an audacious plan, but I worry for the safety of your ships and men."

The admiral smiled. "This old guy has quite a few surprises left in him, ready to be unleashed on the Yamato. Don't worry, young Musado. We will be fine. But be careful: along this stretch of coastline there is a village nearby, nestled right into the mountains. You must avoid it, as the Yamato have taken it over. Even though Tiger's Nest Temple is located in the heart of the mountain range, you will have to go the long way around."

"I think it's quite brilliant," Kyoung said. "And Admiral Yi is the best naval officer in all of the Seven Kingdoms. I have faith in him."

The admiral and his men left the tent, Kyoung walking out with them.

Kwan held Kira back. "I don't like this. Even if you get to Jindo safely, it's a trap. The dragon is leading you right to the temple monks who want to kill you!"

"I have no choice!" Kira snapped.

"Let me go in your stead," Kwan said.

Her eyes widened as she took in her heavily bandaged

brother. "You can hardly stand."

"But they aren't after me—"

Kira shook her head. "This I know in my heart. It must be me. If Sunim were here, he would say the same thing."

Her brother closed his eyes. "I'm scared," he said. "I feel like I might not see my little sister again."

"Don't worry," Jaewon cut in. "I'll be with her."

Kwan gave Jaewon a dirty look. "That's what I'm afraid of."

She was in an underground tunnel, like the ones in Hansong. It was dark and empty and stank to high hell of rot and sewage. But the stench couldn't mask the odor of true evil. There was a demon in the tunnels. And she was on the hunt.

The pitter-patter of small feet caught Kira's attention. She was surprised to see the form of a child up ahead. Its little girl face turned to her and laughed an unnatural high-pitched squeal. Kira saw the telltale shimmer of underworld magic. The demon form underneath the skin taunted her.

Pulling out her bow, Kira took careful aim. Before she could release the arrow, the demon face disappeared and the child looked at her in horror. Tears fell from her eyes as she began to sob.

"Please don't kill me! I'm frightened! I want my mommy!"

Shaken, Kira lowered her bow and stared aghast at the child. She had the strange urge to comfort it. She took one step forward but stopped. Instinct took over and forced her to reconsider.

This was not a child.

She raised her bow again. "I'm not fooled by you, demon."

The child snarled at her with its true demon face. Kira released her arrow but the demon dodged it and raced into the tunnels, Kira close behind. The demon child led her deeper into the tunnels, into total darkness. It was only Kira's tiger vision that let her see where she was going.

The tunnel descended lower until it dead-ended in front of a large black iron door. There was no sign of the child demon. Kira walked the length of the tunnel again, but it was gone. A soft knocking drew her attention back to the door. Without even realizing, Kira found herself in front of it.

The knocking came again, a little louder this time, as if someone or something was trying to communicate with her.

It was an ancient door, thick and strong and bolted by three large metal rods. Whatever was locked away on the other side was meant to never come out.

Still, Kira was drawn to the door even as her gut raged in warning. There was a chittering sound on the other side, then a sudden hushed quiet. An expectant lull as if the creatures were waiting for her. Kira leaned against the door, listening. Only silence. And then whispering voices that spoke to her. Begging her to release them from their imprisonment. To be their savior. The whispering went on and on, filling her head so she heard nothing else. Her hand was compelled to reach for the first latch and rest there. Three pulls and the door would be unlocked, and they would all be free. The whispering reached a fevered pitch, urging her on. But her hand trembled in place, fighting itself as it touched the lever. And then it was immobile. Frozen by the screaming in her head that finally silenced the whispers. It took all her effort and force of mind to drop her hand.

"No," she whispered. "I will not let you out."

At her words, an explosion of shrieks and banging erupted against the door. So loud and so hard that it threatened to beat the door in.

"We will find you and kill you!"

"There is no place you can go to escape from us!"

"You are ours! Our master has promised you to us."

The creatures banged violently against the iron door; so great was their fury that the top bolt broke in half. They howled and raged against the door with even greater violence, causing the second bolt to break. Kira watched in horror as cracks appeared in the third bolt. She rushed forward, bracing the door against the strength of the creatures on the other side.

Over and over the creatures crashed against the door. Kira's hands absorbed the impact as the pain numbed her arms. How long would it take before they broke free? They pounded the iron door relentlessly, finally causing the last bolt to start to bend. How many were behind the door? The chittering sounds sent chills down her spine, and Kira pressed her body weight against the last bolt. Suddenly, the pressure abated and the door was still. Had the creatures given up or would Kira be stuck there forever, protecting this entranceway? Long moments passed. Then a powerful surge rammed itself against the door, shattering the bolt and sending Kira flying into the wall. She watched as the door flew open and screaming dark things poured out, engulfing her.

Kira woke up feeling like she was having a seizure, so painful was the unusual tightness of her chest. The fright of her vision was vivid and real. Something about the creatures scared her more than even the Demon Lord.

She paced the small cabin of Admiral Yi's ship. Looking out the window, she saw that the skies were still dark. Needing a breath of fresh air, she stepped out onto the deck and stood in a quiet corner next to the railing.

They'd left with the evening tide. Jaewon was huddled in the captain's quarters nursing a cup of ginger tea and praying to the heavens that he wouldn't get sick. Admiral Yi also gave Jaewon fresh diced ginger to swallow down every hour. It was an old sailors' trick that the admiral swore would relieve all symptoms of seasickness. Kira knew she should check on her friend, but not yet. She was still too shaken up.

The bracing sea wind was clearing away the last vestiges of her nightmare, but still the fear clung to her. Her visions were not always clear anymore. She didn't understand what they were supposed to mean. In retrospect, she should have known from her weird dreams that Fulang would break through the cave. But it was only afterward that she understood what they'd meant. It would do no good to be late interpreting another vision. She couldn't afford another catastrophe. Now they were sailing to Jindo, where so much danger lay ahead of her. If only she knew what her dreams meant. But nothing made sense anymore. She wished she could see her friend Nara. Perhaps Nara's visions could help her sort through her own. As she thought about her *kumiho* friend, it surprised her how close she had gotten to Nara in such a short time. Nara was the first true female friend that Kira had ever made. She missed the kumiho's feminine strength. In many ways, Nara reminded her of her aunt, Queen Ja-young—both strong, beautiful women with a regal demeanor.

She stared up at the sky and wondered what was happening to her cousin and her little *dokkaebi*. Worry for them gnawed at her stomach. How frightened they must be. She prayed to the heavens that Fulang and the monks would not harm either of them. She prayed that she would be successful.

"I'm so sorry, Taejo. I'm coming for you," she said to the night. "Gom, please take good care of him for me."

Fortunately for Jaewon, the ocean was calm and he was able to sleep for most of the trip. By early evening, they were in sight of Modo Island.

Not far from shore, they lowered the wooden dinghy into the water, and Kira and Jaewon climbed down the side of the ship and dropped into the little boat. The crew passed them their bags, bedrolls, and most important, their full water bags. Kira and Jaewon each picked up an oar and began to row the boat to shore. It was low tide and they were able to make it to Modo quickly.

Once on land, Kira and Jaewon dragged the dinghy into the woods and away from sight. Although Admiral Yi had told them that Modo was uninhabited, Kira wanted to check it out herself to be sure. She left Jaewon setting up camp near where they'd landed and went off to explore the island. It took her less than an hour to survey the entire island. It was dense with tall trees and was quite hilly for such a small island. She spotted plenty of birds but held out no hope for any other game. What the island didn't have were any streams or ponds. Kira could find no signs of running water anywhere.

The northwest side of the island, facing Jindo, was an explosion of color as glorious yellow rape flowers blossomed all along the hills. Kira made sure that they kept well behind the forest line. The admiral had warned them that the Yamato posted patrols along the shoreline of Jindo.

Her keen night vision gave her a clear sight of Jindo. Enemy patrols were stationed at several points along the coast, their lanterns winking in and out in the darkness. If the admiral didn't create a diversion, it would be hard for her and Jaewon to escape the notice of the patrols. Having seen enough, she headed to their campsite, but Jaewon was not there. He'd set up the beginnings of a campfire but had not lit it. She wandered down to the beach, where she found him in the shallows. His shirtsleeves and pants were rolled up as he wrestled with an octopus.

"I'm impressed," she said, clapping her hands together. "That's not an easy feat."

Jaewon smiled. "I live to serve, my lady."

Gathering up a little cooking pot filled with clams and abalone, he beamed at her. "If it's safe to have a fire, I can cook dinner tonight."

"Yes, it'll be fine. This island is so hilly and forested that they wouldn't see anything from this side. But the admiral was right." She sighed. "There's no water source anywhere on the island. You'll have to use our water to cook dinner. I'll put out our bowls to catch rain, if we're lucky, and let's conserve our water until we get to Jindo."

Jaewon agreed. He filled the metal pot he was carrying with seaweed and water from his water bag and returned to their camp. He tucked the pot into a corner of the fire.

That night, they enjoyed a seaweed stew filled with seafood.

"I'm surprised," Kira said. "But that was delicious."

"Why surprised?" Jaewon looked offended. "Seung is not the only one who can cook!"

"Yes, but some of the things you made were not so tasty," she replied.

Jaewon grinned. "Well, I admit that I'm not so good with meat and rice. But I definitely know how to cook seafood," he said. "My mother was originally from a little seashore town in Kaya. She is the reigning champion of seafood cuisine in all of Wagay." His voice petered out as his smile faded.

Kira knew he was thinking of his mother, of how she had tried to kill him when they were in North Wagay Village.

"Well, I am impressed because I can't cook anything," Kira said. "I think there is a talent for cooking that you either have or don't have. And I most certainly don't have it."

Jaewon shook his head at her. "Not true. You roast meats."

"More like burn them," she retorted.

Jaewon shrugged. "I like my meat well done."

Kira gave him a disbelieving look.

He smiled back. "Cooking, like anything else, can be learned. Even the worst cooks can eventually make simple yet flavorful meals. I think the truth is you don't *want* to cook. You are one of those people who just want to eat the food and not make it."

"That is very true," Kira said complacently.

They finished eating in contented silence. The sound of the gentle waves coming in and out was peaceful.

"You know what I like best about this island?" Jaewon asked.

Kira cocked an eyebrow at him.

"Your brother is not here." He grinned.

"I thought you liked Kwan."

"I do," Jaewon said. "But he is always hanging around so I can't be alone with you."

"He is very smart, my brother," Kira teased. "He recognizes a lecher."

Jaewon was insulted. "How dare you! I'm no lecher!"

With a snicker, Kira pulled out her blanket and laid it next to the fire. It was so easy to joke around with Jaewon. He was a comfort to her.

As she settled herself, she worried about Taejo and Gom. She wondered what was happening to them. If they were eating and how scared they probably were. She needed to get to Jindo as quickly as possible. If only the pathway would appear, it would take far less time to run the miracle bridge than to row over to the island.

"What are you thinking of?" Jaewon asked.

"I'm hoping that this magic path opens up at the right time," she said. "I'd rather run than row."

"Yes, but I'd rather row than drown, thank you very much."

Jaewon unfurled his blanket and lay down on the opposite side of the fire. "What do you think about the admiral's crazy plan?"

"Kyoung Oppa thinks it's brilliant," she said, "so I'm sure it will work. Hopefully, all the patrols will be called away and we can sneak across."

"Maybe it would be better if we take the boat over," he said.

"We'll see," Kira said, her eyes closing. "My concern is that we need to take advantage of the initial chaos when the patrols will desert their posts. Rowing would take a long time. But let's get some sleep. I want to wake up early and try to collect morning dew for water."

"How do you do that?" Jaewon asked.

"I'll show you tomorrow." With a tired yawn, Kira fell fast asleep.

It was nighttime. She was standing outside a large encampment full of soldiers. Her body was rigid, her teeth grinding down on each other. With all her might, she willed herself desperately not to move, but she was no longer in charge. An overriding compulsion forced her to enter the campsite and walk through. As she passed the soldiers, they greeted her with respectful bows. But she took no notice of them. Struggling mentally against the force that was controlling her, Kira was in a panic. She had the same sense of invasiveness she'd had when Nara had shared her memories. But this time the intrusion was by a malignant force that overpowered her. She moved as if in a waking nightmare, aware of her actions but powerless to stop herself. Sweat beaded her forehead. Kira tried to open her mouth and scream, but her lips wouldn't move. Only her legs kept going, cutting through the Iron Army, leading her to the command center. This would be where her brothers were.

She tried to stop herself, but the intruder was like a vise in her head. With mounting dread, Kira knew that she was being forced to do something horrible. Her left hand swept the entrance curtain aside as her right hand gripped her sword. Inside, her brothers were both huddled over a map with several other generals. They looked up at her approach, first with smiles and then with growing confusion. She dispatched the generals first, before they could even register the attack.

"Kira, what's wrong?" Kyoung asked, his eyes wide with alarm. "Can you hear me? Are you still our sister?"

Kwan circled around Kyoung with his sword drawn. It tore at Kira's heart to see the agony in his face.

"What have you done to our sister?" he shouted.

Finally a slip by the intruder, a lessening of the vise grip on her head. "Help me," she croaked out in a harsh voice. "Kill me now before I kill you both!"

As soon as the words were released, the viselike hold gripped her again. And then Kira realized her mistake. She'd paralyzed her brothers. Inside her head, she shrieked in horror, desperately battling the intruder, but her body wouldn't listen. In their momentary confusion at hearing their sister's voice, Kira attacked them both. First she felled her eldest brother, her sword slashing across his neck. Without losing any momentum, her sword swung down next onto Kwan's arm, severing it.

Kwan stared at her in horror.

"No, Kira. No!" His words choked on a death rattle as Kira stabbed him through his gut. She heard an evil laugh filling her head and recognized it as the Demon Lord's.

And then she was screaming, her mind freed at last.

Harsh cries tore from her throat as Jaewon shook her awake. For a moment, she didn't know where she was. It was still dark out but for the stars glinting in the inky sky.

"It's all right, it's just a dream," he said soothingly. "Hush now, it's not real."

Broken sobs shook her body as she clung to him. It had felt so real. The foreign intrusion into her head. The absolute control over her mind and body, forcing her to kill her brothers. This was not a vision that could ever come true. She was never going to let this happen. She would kill herself first.

She wept for a long time, unable to speak of her vision. But Jaewon never pressed for details, only holding her in his arms, providing her comfort and solace. She finally fell asleep, still wrapped tightly in his embrace.

In the morning, Kira woke up in Jaewon's arms. His face rested against the top of her head. He was sound asleep, his breath tickling the back of her neck. Kira freed herself gently, careful not to wake him. She needed some private moments alone.

She gathered her things and walked up the mountain so as not to be disturbed. She used a small amount of water from her water bag to wipe her face and clean her teeth. She held a cold wet cloth against her eyes, feeling how swollen they were from all of her crying. The mere thought of her nightmare caused her to shake once again. Pure unadulterated fear shot through her body. This was worse than when she'd heard the voice of the Demon

Lord talking to her constantly.

She tried to push the vision from her head and returned to camp. Jaewon lay sleeping. His face in repose was so young and carefree. The sadness that she'd associated with him for so long had mostly disappeared. There was a lightness about him that hadn't been there before. She hoped she'd never see that deep sadness within him again. And yet, she worried for him. She didn't want to be the one to hurt him again. He meant too much to her.

Waking Jaewon, she showed him how to collect dew. There had been no rain overnight, so their bowls were empty. Kira walked over to a large open field of grass and began to wipe the blades with a clean rag. They were moist with dew. She then squeezed her rag into her bowl. Within ten minutes, her bowl was full. They collected enough to fill their metal pot. After gathering more firewood, Jaewon lit a fire to boil the water.

"You can only collect the dew in the early morning, while it is still cool," she said.

"Clever trick," he said. "Who taught you that?"

"My father," Kira said. "All my survival lessons came from him. He would take us hiking into the mountains to hunt and teach us everything he knew about nature."

"He sounds like a great man."

Kira nodded. "The best," she said simply. "I miss him every day."

Jaewon reached over and enfolded Kira in his arms.

"You helped me reunite with my father, and I thank you for that," he said.

"I didn't do anything," she mumbled into his chest.

He squeezed her tight. "Yes, you did! I wouldn't have had the courage to seek out my parents if I hadn't met you. I would still be running away from my problems. But now I feel like I have my father back, and to hear you talk about missing yours breaks my heart," he said. "I know he's not like your father, but I would gladly share mine with you. And I know he would embrace you like the daughter he never had."

Kira snorted. "That sounded suspiciously like a back-handed proposal." She pushed away and sat down, arms folded as she gave him the stink eye.

A flush crept up his neck and into his cheeks as he sat across from her.

"I'm not trying to insult you," he said. "I feel closer to you than anyone else in the world. I have felt so lost for a long time. Yet when I'm with you, I feel I've found my way. You're the reason I can make it through the day. Your face is the one I see when I fall asleep at night. And the only one I want to wake up to in the morning."

Jaewon rose up to his knees and moved closer, bringing his face inches away from Kira's. He threaded his fingers through her short, thick hair and stared into her eyes with an intensity that brought a sharp ache to her chest and uncomfortable heat everywhere else. His action shocked her into stillness. She couldn't deny her attraction and the desperate desire for another kiss. His lips hovered out of reach for a long moment, causing her body to sway forward and bring her lips to his. The warmth of his mouth brought a tingling to her navel that spread rapidly through her body.

His hands, which had been holding her tightly, began to wander the length of her body. Kira recoiled violently and punched Jaewon in the face.

"How dare you!"

"That was an accident," he said, rubbing his sore chin. "I didn't mean to do it! I just lost my head—"

"You'll lose something for sure if you try that again," Kira said through gritted teeth. She jumped to her feet and stomped away in a rage mixed with the mortification of knowing she'd enjoyed his caresses.

Awkward and uncomfortable, Kira stayed away from Jaewon and spent the day hunting and digging for water. It took all afternoon, but she was able to dig out a small well and see it fill with groundwater. Filling her water bags, she returned to camp with two birds she'd caught.

Jaewon sat beside the fire, whittling away at a piece of wood. "What have you been doing all day?" he asked.

Ignoring him, Kira quickly cleaned her kill and prepared a makeshift spit that she placed over the fire.

Jaewon rose suddenly and came up behind her, hugging her tight around her waist.

"Don't be mad at me," he mumbled into her hair. "I

hate it when you're mad."

Kira sighed and tried to shake him off. "You're always saying that! Let go!"

"No, I won't! Not until you stop being mad at me," he replied.

Kira turned her head and held Jaewon's gaze. "I said let go," she repeated in a quiet voice.

Jaewon released her immediately. "I'm sorry," he said.

Kira could see his sincerity and the bubble of anger in her heart dissipated. "I'm not mad. I just find you irritating."

Jaewon grinned and slid in front of her again. "Now I can tell you aren't mad anymore."

Kira sighed.

Laughing, Jaewon planted a light kiss on her lips.

"Argh! Cut it out! You're worse than Jindo." She swatted him away.

Jaewon dodged her blow and ran to the other side of the fire. "There you go insulting me again," he said. "Now I'm like a dog."

"Jindo's cuter," she retorted, hiding her grin.

"But my kisses are nicer, aren't they?"

"I don't know—you both slobber the same amount."

"No I don't! Here, let me show you!" He started to come closer.

Kira glared at the laughing boy. "Don't you dare."

Jaewon sat down with an exaggerated huff and made a sorrowful face.

Kira bit the inside of her mouth to keep from laughing,

and turned her attention to the fire, where the meat was beginning to burn on one side. Part of her was thrilled by his touch and his nearness. She didn't want to admit it, but she liked his kisses. But he was too much of a distraction.

Kira kept an eye on Jaewon as she finished roasting the meat. Taking out a small battered teapot, he placed it in the corner of the fire and brewed barley tea.

When the meat was done, she served the meal. They sat across from each other, Jaewon leaning against a fallen log while Kira rested her head on the mossy rock behind her.

"I'm not good at foraging so I didn't find anything extra for dinner," she said.

"This is a feast," Jaewon said.

Kira snorted. "Rice, I would kill for some rice."

"But for that, this is a perfect feast," he said.

They ate silently. Kira stared out into the ocean, watching the last of the sun's rays glittering over the waves.

"He's safe," Jaewon said. He knew she was thinking of Taejo. "Gom is keeping him safe for you."

Kira missed the little dokkaebi but was glad that he was with Taejo. She was grateful that he'd sacrificed himself to go with Taejo. It was as if Gom had known that being with Taejo was the one thing she would have wanted him to do. She prayed that he was all right.

Jaewon sat by the fire, carving a small piece of wood with his knife.

“What are you making now?” Kira asked.

“I’ve been trying to capture Gom, but I can’t quite get him right,” he said. “I keep making him more gruesome than cute.”

He showed her the little face he’d carved into the wood. Kira laughed. “It looks more like something from my nightmares,” she said.

Jaewon rubbed absently at a callus on one of his fingers. “My father is really good at carving these cute little animal figurines,” he said. “I was always asking him for the scary tigers and bears and monsters. But my brother loved the cute ones.”

He paused. “When we were at North Wagay, I asked if he was carving again. But he creates more artistic stuff now. I should have asked him to teach me how to do cute ones. Then I could get Gom’s face right.”

Kira didn’t respond, letting him talk uninterrupted. He spoke easily and with clear affection for his father. Unlike the awkwardness that would arise when he mentioned his mother. Not that she blamed him. It was hard to even think of the insane woman she’d met in North Wagay as Jaewon’s mother.

“Maybe I should give it up and stick to carving dogs,” he finally said as he leaned back with a sigh. “You want to try?”

Kira shook her head. “I have no artistic talent at all. When my mother tried to teach me to embroider and paint, she realized quickly that it was not my forte. I’m very efficient. I can sew straight and evenly. But I seem to be missing the ability to create beauty."

"Why don't you try? Even if it's bad, the effort of it can be quite calming," Jaewon said.

As she opened her mouth to say no, a vision of Taejo flashed before her eyes. She felt the worry and guilt start to rise within her again. Wondering how he was and how the monks were treating him. Just the thought of Fulang started to make her blood boil. She stood up abruptly and went to sit by Jaewon's side. The idea of carving something suddenly appealed to her. It was a much-needed distraction.

"Show me," she said.

They spent the second night on the island carving up wood and talking in contented friendship. For once in her life, Kira felt completely relaxed with someone not a member of her family. As he showed her the intricate cuts he would make into his carving, Kira spent more time gazing at his expressive face, enjoying the play of firelight that lit his eyes with warmth. She loved the way his dimples would flash in and out with his words. The one on his left cheek was a deep indentation that made her want to poke her finger into it.

"Are you listening to me or are you too busy admiring my beauty?" Jaewon asked.

"Something about your face makes me sleepy," she said.

"I'm not sure if that was an insult or a strange compliment," he remarked.

Chuckling, Kira set her blanket beside the fire and yawned. "It's a good thing. You are very relaxing," she said. Closing her eyes, she felt Jaewon lean over and brush her hair from her face.

"I wish I could say the same about you," he said. "I'm fairly sure you're going to give me a heart attack."

"At least I will never bore you," she said, before she fell asleep.

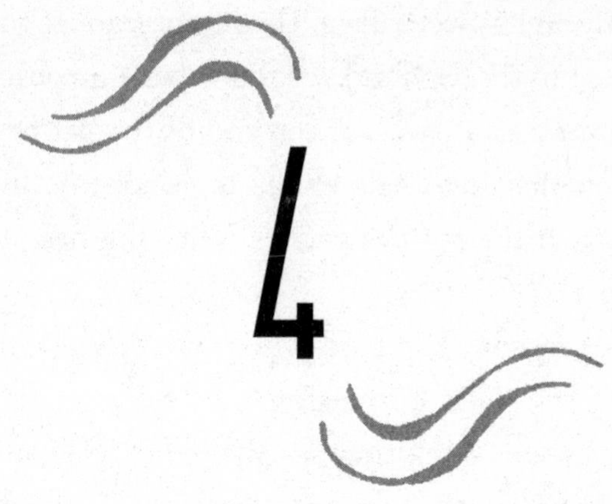

On the fourth day since the dragon had kidnapped Taejo and Gom, and their third day on the island, Kira and Jaewon packed up their bags and remained hidden in the brush on the northwest side of the island.

That evening they watched the path appear. The sun was low in the sky as patches of the wide muddy path peeked through the water. Kira studied the path, the twists and turns. She wanted to make sure there would be no surprises. They had only six more days to get to the Tiger's Nest Temple.

Right at dusk, they began to see the beginning of the phenomenon. A faint glimpse of black sand peeked through the turquoise waves. Then the seas parted and a sandy path slowly appeared between the two islands. Several torches were lit on the Jindo shore as the patrols switched to the night crew. From what Kira observed and the admiral had told her, the end of the pathway would open on the Jindo side closer to where the mountains began. Fortunately, the patrols were congregated several li away.

Half an hour had passed and the fading sunlight still marked the horizon, making the widening sandy path clearer to see. "Can't they see the path?" Jaewon asked.

"Not unless they know to look for it," Kira said. "The path is dark and they aren't close enough."

Anxious, they waited some more.

"If we don't go soon, the tide will get us," Kira said.

Jaewon looked at the vast ocean surrounding them. "Can't you use the tidal stone to keep the tide away?"

"I wish it was that easy," she said. "As soon as I use it, the stone will heat up and shine brightly. I don't want to risk being caught."

"And I don't want to risk drowning," Jaewon said.

"I promise I won't let that happen," Kira replied.

She eyed the streaks of sunlight still shimmering over the horizon. She cast Jaewon a grim look. "Let's go."

They strapped their bags onto their backs and headed down the pathway. Just then they heard a muted roar and screaming. The tiny figures of the Yamato patrol were racing down the beach, away from their exit point. Fire blazed in the darkening sky, smoke billowing into the air.

Something was burning just beyond their vision.

This was what they'd been waiting for. Kira and Jaewon ran.

By now, the pathway was wide enough for a company of men to walk on. With the last vestiges of sunlight behind them, they set a hard pace down the sea road. Night had finally fallen. Whatever distraction Admiral Yi had set up was working. She watched the Jindo shore. There were no signs of the patrols. Thanking the admiral for his help, she urged Jaewon to run faster. For now their biggest enemy was the tide.

The moon was covered with clouds and the night was dark, but the black path glinted with the pearly shards of broken shells.

"This is beautiful," Jaewon said. "One day I hope we can walk this path again and really enjoy it."

Kira didn't answer. It was lovely and unreal. In another life it would have been nice to walk the sea road with Jaewon. But right now, all her thoughts were on saving Taejo.

Part of her was irritated at Jaewon and the other part was sad. The beauty of the night, the miracle of the path, none of it was important to her. She didn't have the luxury of time to appreciate the glories of nature. She needed only to use it for her goal.

"No more talking," she said. "We need to be quiet."

They ran in silence, with only the pitter-patter of their boots and the lapping water indicating their passage down the miracle road. The path began narrowing.

The water lapped gently along the sides, sometimes rushing up enough to wet their feet. Past the halfway mark to Jindo, the tide began to return. The water rushed over their feet, slowing them down.

"We've got to move faster," Kira said.

She was flying over the water but soon saw Jaewon falling behind. When she slowed down to let him catch up, the tide swept over the entire path. They found themselves slogging in ankle-high water before it receded.

"Push yourself harder!" Kira urged Jaewon.

They were nearing the shoreline of Jindo Island when the path disappeared completely. The ocean had returned with a vengeance. They'd run out of time.

Kira gripped the tidal stone through its bag against her chest. She risked calling down the entire Yamato patrol if she used it.

"No!" she said through gritted teeth. "I will not fail today!"

Powering through the rising tide, Kira moved forward, but Jaewon couldn't keep up. She reached behind and grasped his hand.

"Come on, Kim Jaewon!" she said. "We're almost there."

He gripped her tightly and gave her a solemn nod, his energy renewed. The tide was to their knees now and it took all their energy to cut through the waves. A sudden surge took Kira by surprise, knocking her off her feet. Only Jaewon's strong grip kept her from being swept away. He wrapped his arm around her waist and carried her through the churning ocean until she regained her footing. Digging her feet into the shifting sands, Kira barreled forward. This time it was Jaewon who fell. Kira wrapped both her arms around him, and put all her might into forcing her legs to cut through the waves. Instead of lifting her feet, she shuffled and slid forward, holding on to Jaewon, who weakened with each step. They closed in on the shore, their arms linked in a vise-like grip. After only a few minutes, that felt like hours, they finally reached dry land.

Kira immediately looked around for the Yamato patrols, but the beach was empty. Jaewon started to sit but Kira pulled him forward. "No, let's get out of sight first."

Exhausted, they headed into the thickly wooded forest. Kira kept them moving for almost an hour. She tracked the terrain with her keen night vision. Although the mountains were to their right, there were far too many villages all along the foothills. Kira forced them deeper into the island and the forests, away from the mountains, until she found a small running stream. Only then did she allow Jaewon to collapse.

"My legs are burning," Jaewon complained. "My body hurts and I'm cold."

"You need to change out of those wet things," Kira said.

Jaewon raised his arms across his chest in mock modesty, a comical look of outrage on his face.

"Not in front of me," she said.

With a huff, he dragged himself into the bushes, causing Kira to let out a tired laugh.

She changed quickly into her spare clothes and hung her wet things on the bushes to dry. But her blanket that had been rolled up on top of her pack was soaking wet. Sighing, she threw it over a low-hanging tree branch. Walking tenderly on her bare feet, she gathered up wood and twigs to start a fire. By the time it was started, Jaewon had returned. He threw his clothes and his blanket across the tops of some dense bushes and dropped down in front of the fire.

"Is it safe to light a fire?" he asked.

Kira nodded. "We are pretty deep in the jungle. The Yamato patrols are on the coastline and the northern side of the island. We're safe for now."

"Thank the heavens! It gets cold at night and my blanket is a bit wet."

Kira motioned to hers. "Hopefully not as wet as mine."

Jaewon grinned. "I'm happy to share my blanket with you."

"I'll be fine without one," she said with a glare.

"Are you sure? My blanket is only a little wet."

She ignored him.

He sighed. "Our boots are not going to dry by morning."

Kira finished prepping the fire and then gathered four long sticks. Rummaging through her bag, she pulled out a length of hemp cloth and ripped it into four squares. After shaking the boots out, she shoved the cloth into the bottom of each pair. She then stabbed the sticks deep into the ground near the fire and hung their boots upside down on each stick.

Jaewon gazed at her in openmouthed admiration.

"Why have I never thought to do that?" he asked.

"Women are smarter than men," she teased.

"I've come to believe that is true," he said. "So where is the nearest village? I know how much you are dying for some rice."

Kira shook her head. "We must avoid the villages—there will be Yamato patrols in all of them. We head straight for the Tiger's Nest Temple."

"So that's why we're heading west, away from the mountains. You're seeking a more isolated approach to the temple. But how will we know where we're going?"

Kira gritted her teeth hard. "I can smell the dragon's magic from here," she said. "It's mixed with whatever spells the monks are using to protect its boundaries. It's a stench I can't ignore."

With a comical look, Jaewon leaned over and smelled his own armpit. "It's not me, is it?"

"No, don't worry, you only stink a little."

"Excuse me! I'll have you know you don't smell too pretty yourself," he said.

"Good, I'll stink some more so maybe you'll stay away from me," she retorted.

He scratched his head and sidled closer to her. "Actually, I don't have a very strong sense of smell, you know. Not like you." He leaned in to take a whiff of her neck, causing her to stiffen and shove him away.

"Ow! I was trying to smell you to see if you stink," he complained with a laugh. "You're always so rough with me. My delicate skin is all bruised and battered because of you."

"Such a liar," Kira said, clicking her tongue in disapproval.

"I'm serious!" He untied his jacket and pulled up his shirt, revealing a lean, sculpted abdomen. "Here, see? All these bruises are because of you."

Kira inhaled sharply and averted her eyes, but not before getting a good look at his lean and well-muscled torso.

"You are the biggest baby. That doesn't look like bruises, they look like dirt. You should do a better job when you bathe."

"Dirt?" Jaewon sputtered. He grabbed her hand and rubbed it against his stomach. "That's not dirt, see? It doesn't rub off!"

Kira jumped in shock, all her senses tingling at the feel of his bare skin. Her cheeks were inflamed with a fiery heat. Unnerved and angry at her reaction, she pinched at the smooth skin under her fingertips. Jaewon yelped and flinched away.

"That's going to leave another bruise, you evil girl," he complained, rubbing at his sore spot.

"And you would deserve it." Ignoring his complaints, Kira took out her weapons and checked them over carefully, worried that they might have gotten wet during the crossing. Her bow and arrows were fine and her sword still dry in its leather sheath. She rose to her feet and headed out to hunt for game.

"You're going to go without your boots?" Jaewon asked in surprise.

Kira smirked at him. "Makes me extra sneaky."

"Maybe I should go with you," he said, rising to his feet. "Hey, wait for me!"

She turned and watched him step gingerly on the ground, swearing as he stubbed his toe on a rock. His awkwardness was surprisingly endearing. It left her with a warmth in her chest that she was getting used to feeling around him.

"You're going to scare away all the game," she said.

"Wait, don't leave me alone. What if a wild animal gets me?"

"So pathetic," Kira sighed.

"You'll be sorry if a tiger eats me," he whined.

Kira shook her head. "If a tiger ate you, it would be because you're so noisy. It's like you're banging a drum and shouting 'dinnertime, come eat me!'"

Jaewon sat back down and crossed his arms. For all his complaining, she could see how tired he was.

"Cruel girl," he muttered.

Kira smiled at his sulking face. "*Ya,* Kim Jaewon. Be quiet or all you'll get for dinner is slugs."

She laughed at the horrified look on his face as she turned and left the campsite.

In the morning, Jaewon was up first, preparing their meal. He'd taken the early morning watch and had gathered roots and vegetables and even caught three wild chickens.

"I got enough here to tide us over for the day," he said. "As long as you don't eat too much."

Kira shot him an offended glare, which made him chuckle.

"Let's face it, you have a healthy appetite," he said. "I think you eat more than I do."

"So?" she asked coldly.

"Nothing! I, um, never mind."

"I eat a lot because I work hard and I burn a lot of energy," she said. "A healthy appetite is a sign of a healthy body. If I eat more than you, maybe it's because you're too lazy."

"I'm sorry if you took my words the wrong way. I take it that this is a sore point for you . . ."

Kira heaved a long sigh. "I see women give these confusing messages all the time. Urging the men to enjoy their food and eat a lot, and telling their girls to go hungry or else they'll get fat and no man will want to marry them.

"My appetite was a big joke with the court ladies. Even my aunt, the queen, would criticize me when I ate with her," Kira said. "It got to the point where I would eat nothing because her constant criticisms would make me lose my appetite. But my mother always brought me food afterward. She never judged, she only ever loved me."

The pain threatened to overwhelm her and she closed her eyes, holding back her tears. She could see her mother sliding open the door to her quarters, carrying a full tray of food with her own hands. No servants to help her. She could hear her mom's voice in her head, telling her:

"Never go to bed hungry, my child. Always fill your stomach so you can be strong. So much stronger than I ever was."

Her mother would sit beside her as she ate. Patting Kira's hair from time to time, urging her to eat all her favorite foods.

"I love to watch you eat," she said as she stacked up the empty dishes. "You eat with such enjoyment and pleasure. I love how you find comfort and happiness in the simple things of life. Never forget them. Never forget what makes you happy."

The memory faded and Kira was left again with the aching loss that always overwhelmed her when she thought of her mother.

Jaewon was kneeling in front of her, patting her hands between his.

"I meant no harm by my words," he said. "I'm always teasing you, but I never mean to hurt you. Forgive me."

Kira looked up at him. "I know that. I was missing my mother," she said.

Jaewon's eyes turned sad. "Me too."

He put an arm around her. She leaned against his shoulder and rested.

After a long moment, he asked. "Hungry?"

She nodded.

"Good," he said, rising to his feet.

Kira watched as Jaewon placed a generous portion of food in her wooden bowl before passing it to her.

"Watching you eat is the highlight of my day," he said with a smile. "Don't ever change."

His words were so similar to what her mother used to say that Kira had to blink back her tears.

"Don't worry," she said, her voice husky with emotion. "I won't."

In the heart of the island, the jungle seemed nearly untouched by humans. There were no villages to avoid and no fear of running into any Yamato patrols. Kira finally began to circle around toward the eastern mountain range.

It was early afternoon on the fifth day since Fulang took Taejo. Finally, they saw what they'd been looking for. In a valley of gently sloping mountains, the tremendous height of one craggy cliff towered over all the rest. Where the lower surrounding mountains were green and filled with color, the black rock was devoid of any vegetation. A rocky crag on which nothing grew. But high in the shadows of the mountain, Kira observed the shape and glow of the golden temple. It stood in stark contrast to the darkness of its mountain. Tiger's Nest Temple was built into the cliffs itself with no discernible entrance into it.

Suddenly they heard the roars of an angry animal.

"That sounds like a tiger," Jaewon said. His eyebrows furrowed in concern. "What's it doing on an island?"

Kira had frozen in shock, trying to place where the roars were coming from. "Tigers are great swimmers," she said absently. "They've been spotted swimming to the islands from the mainland."

The bellows swept over them again. Trying to pinpoint the location, Kira began to head farther inland. The tiger's roars were echoing all around them, making it hard to figure out where they were coming from. But Kira was determined to try.

"Why are we heading toward the tiger?" Jaewon asked as he hurried to keep pace with her. "Shouldn't we be running away from it?"

Kira didn't answer, concentrating on following the anguished cries.

"Also, you do realize we're going the wrong way, right? We are heading to the other side of the island."

Kira continued to ignore him, focused on saving the animal in need. Finally she spotted an open clearing where a large hole had been camouflaged with bamboo and foliage, which the weight of the tiger had collapsed.

The tiger had fallen along the side of the pit wall, but it looked as if it had been skewered through the side by one of the numerous sharpened bamboo sticks within the trap.

Without hesitating, Kira began to climb into the pit.

"What are you doing?" Jaewon seized her by the upper arm. "You're gonna get yourself killed!"

Kira bit back an angry retort when she saw the terror on his face.

"Trust me," she said.

Jaewon's face was tortured, but he gave her a terse nod and let go. She lowered herself into the pit, carefully avoiding the bamboo spears. Once down, she hacked away at several spears that were in her way. The tiger was watching her through slitted eyes.

Reaching the tiger's side, Kira noticed that a slivered part of a spear had pierced through its armpit and out its shoulder. The tiger didn't move or make a sound. As she reached for the spear, the tiger licked her hand, as if in gratitude.

"Don't worry," Kira said. "I'll get you out of here."

Kira grasped the bamboo and swiftly removed it. The tiger rumbled in pain. Untying her water bag, she poured water over the wound and then inspected it for splinters. Seeing none, she removed her sash and quickly wrapped it around the wound.

She then began to look for a way out of the trap. Reaching over to the other side, she pulled out the unbroken bamboo spears and began to stab them into the side of the pit in ascending order. Stepping lightly on the spears, close to the wall, she made a makeshift staircase. Out of the pit, she turned and whistled to the tiger. Cradling its injured leg to its side, the tiger surged up the flimsy ladder, barely making it as the spears cracked under its weight. Once out of the pit, the tiger collapsed at Kira's feet. She sat and cradled its large head, stroking its fur and wishing her tiger spirit would come and heal it.

"We'll camp here for the night," she said.

Jaewon didn't question her, not even mentioning that it was still quite light to be making camp. Instead, he stared in wary surprise at their unexpected companion.

"Are we going to feed the tiger too?" he asked, moving slowly around the other two. "I don't want to be mistaken for its next meal."

"Don't worry," she said, stroking the tiger's head. "It won't hurt us. I promise."

"I trust you, but not the tiger."

As she inspected the tiger's wounds, she noted that there were numerous puncture wounds across the now blood-matted fur. Opening her bag, she pulled out the small leather bag filled with the salve Shaman Won had given her at North Wagay Village. She spread the pungent herbal medicine over each of the tiger's wounds. In gratitude, the tiger licked Kira's face, tickling her.

Kira glared at the tiger pit. "That is just cruel and awful," she said.

"Well, you can't blame the villagers," Jaewon said. "Tigers are dangerous to most normal people, of which you are not. Normal, I mean."

"But it's strange," she said. "There aren't any villages nearby."

"No, it makes sense to me," he replied. "This must be part of the tiger's territory. So they built a trap where they'd be sure to catch it."

Kira frowned. "There should be no reason for the tiger to bother them if they stay out of each other's territory," she said. "The problem with people is that they are greedy. Trespassing into places they shouldn't and killing off all the game."

"People have to eat too," Jaewon said mildly. "It's not like life is easy for them either."

Kira was in no mood for his opinion. Ignoring him, she sat by the injured tiger's side and murmured softly into its ear. The tiger purred in response, nestling next to Kira as if it were a mere cat.

Jaewon sighed. "I should be used to strange things by now." He scanned the area and shook his head. "I don't think we are safe here."

A deep and menacing growl began to rumble from the tiger's throat. It was chilling to hear. Kira felt the churning of her gut in response. She slid out from under the tiger and grabbed her sword. She beckoned for Jaewon to gather their things and hide within the dense foliage of a large red-flowered camellia bush. The tiger limped over with them. Moments later, a Yamato patrol appeared through the woods.

Two Yamatos appeared, arguing with each other. From Kira's viewpoint, they looked more frightened than anything else. But it was the third soldier coming up behind them that Kira focused on. The shimmer of demon magic gave him away as did the stench that permeated the entire area. Stronger than the wild animal musk of the tiger.

When the two Yamato soldiers saw the empty pit, they began to point and yell in excited tones. The demon soldier seemed to snap. He drew out his sword and killed both soldiers with one movement. As the bodies fell, two black pools of ooze formed out of the ground. In an instant, the soldiers were covered with undulating black masses that were slowly beginning to transform.

Kira had never witnessed an actual possession occur. She watched as one of the black figures latched itself onto the neck of the soldier. At first, she didn't realize what was happening and then comprehension struck her. It was liquefying the internal organs and skeletal mass of the body and consuming it, like a spider. The black ooze was bulking up and materializing as the human body flattened. When there was nothing left but skin, the now fully materialized black figure let itself slither into the skin. The demon was now fully formed into a human.

Kira sprang into action. She reached for her bow and nodded grimly at Jaewon. They both released their arrows at the same time, taking out the newly formed demons as they rose to their feet. The remaining demon bolted. Suddenly, the tiger surged forward. Even with an injured leg, it was faster than the demon. In three bounds, the tiger leaped onto the demon's back and mauled it brutally with its claws. With one swipe of its paw, the tiger ripped the demon's throat out, releasing the black form within from the human skin.

Stepping out into the clearing, Kira and Jaewon approached the deflating bodies, black ooze disappearing into the earth. The tiger limped over to Kira's side. There was no blood or other matter on its muzzle or claws. Kira scratched its head, admiring the cleanness of its kill.

"You know, a tiger would be a great companion to have during a demon attack," Jaewon mused.

Kira had already walked over to the human remains and began to drag one over to the tiger pit. She threw it in the pit and then repeated the action with the other two bodies. When she was done, she looked down in distaste.

"We need to fill this in," she stated. Pulling out her sword, she hacked at the nearby trees, cutting down large leafy branches. Over an hour later, the pit was more than halfway filled with woodland debris. The tiger had been lying in the shade of a nearby tree, watching them through its large yellow eyes.

"That should do it," Kira said. "Hopefully it will stop another tiger from being injured."

"Great, but is it OK if we don't make camp here?" Jaewon asked. "I'm still a little freaked out by what we saw."

"Me too," Kira said. "It was disgusting."

"That goes down on my list of things I wish I'd never seen," Jaewon said.

As if understanding them, the tiger limped forward, leading them away from the horrors of the pit. After a short hike, it brought them into a beautiful meadow with a small but fast-running creek of clear, fresh water. It collapsed by a large rock and stretched out.

"Much better," Jaewon declared.

"No fire," Kira said. "Just in case."

They ate a cold meal of the leftovers Jaewon had saved. Kira shared her food with the tiger, who licked her hand gratefully.

"We'll have to leave early to make up for lost time," Jaewon said.

"No, not until she's better," Kira replied.

"It's a girl?" Jaewon asked in surprise. "I won't ask how you found that out."

Kira slept by the tiger's side and woke in the early hours of the morning to a stunning sight. All around them there lay at least a hundred tigers. She sat up and rubbed her eyes, then caught sight of Jaewon, standing guard nearby, his face filled with wary awe.

"When did this happen?" she asked.

"They've been coming all through the night," he replied. "First one would appear, then another."

"Why didn't you wake me?" she asked.

"You looked so peaceful. As soon as I realized that they had no intention of eating me, I figured I was safe, as long as I stayed close to you. They've just been lying there, patiently waiting."

"Waiting for what?" she asked. She rose to her feet. At that moment all the tigers stood up and roared.

Jaewon looked at her with such a harried expression

that Kira had to laugh. She felt euphoric. Here she stood before an army of tigers, and she was unafraid.

The injured tiger pawed at her side. Kira turned and checked the tiger's wounds. They looked better. The tiger would be fine.

Kira caressed the tiger's head, laughing at the rough texture of her tongue as she licked Kira's hand.

"You are going to wash up now, right?" Jaewon said with a disgusted snort.

"Will it keep you from kissing me?"

"No," he replied immediately.

"Then I might as well wash up."

The tiger let out a loud purr and then sauntered away. One by one, the other tigers all vanished into the morning mist.

Jaewon shivered. "That was eerily strange and scary."

"You were never in danger," Kira replied.

"Tell that to my heart," he retorted, clutching his chest. "I've never been so stressed out in my life!"

Kira studied him with a slight smile. "Are you sure you don't have some actor's blood in you? You're quite good at being overdramatic."

"I'm not acting!" Jaewon looked offended. "Unlike you, things actually scare me."

He started packing up their small camp, muttering a litany of complaints that made Kira snicker.

She left him talking to himself and followed the creek downstream, for privacy. Not too far away she came upon a small pond hidden within the trees. She pulled out her soap and took off her jacket, washing up as quickly as possible. She shivered against the cool morning air, sitting in nothing but her bust wrap and trousers. She ran a comb through her short hair until it crackled. As she wiped her face, she sat staring at her reflection. The scar on her face had faded to a thin white line. She hardly even noticed it anymore. Gazing into the water, she wondered what it was that Jaewon found attractive about her. But for her yellow eyes, she thought her face was nothing special. A narrow face and high cheekbones with a jaw that was a little too angular and lips that were a little too big. Even her shoulders were strong and wide and not narrow and rounded. Not that any of this troubled her. After years of being told how hideous and frightening she looked, she didn't really care about her appearance. But she was genuinely curious to know what about her he seemed to like.

Something was glinting in the depths of the running water. She knelt closer, and an eerie, disturbing feeling crept up her spine as she tried to recognize what she saw. She blinked as she lowered her face closer to the water. The glint was growing larger. Mesmerized by it, she kept staring until she suddenly realized what it was. The milky white of a large fishy-looking eye. Before she could move, a foul creature leaped at her and wrapped its long slimy arms around her neck, trying to drag her into the water.

With a garbled yell, Kira reared back, barely keeping from toppling into the pond. She smelled the evil fishy stink of it. Seizing the monster by the waist, she yanked it out of the water and hurled it away. It landed with a hiss and immediately crawled on all fours back toward her. Kira pulled out her sword and held it at its neck. Immediately it curled over onto itself, shaking in fear.

It spoke in a foreign language that Kira recognized as Yamato.

"Are you a creature of Yamato? What are you doing here? Do you understand me?"

The creature nodded vigorously. "Yes, I speak the language of the Seven Kingdoms," it said. "Please don't kill me. I meant no harm. I was merely curious."

"Oh, no harm at all," Kira sneered. "You only meant to drown me."

"No drowning, just swimming." The creature smiled evilly, creeping ever closer.

Kira stopped its progress with a swipe of her sword. She studied its form carefully. Greenish-gray scales covered its entire body, and its misshapen limbs were attached to its torso in an odd configuration. But the strangest feature was the top of its head, which was concave like a bowl and was brimming with water.

"You don't smell like a demon. What are you?"

"I'm a *kappa*," it replied. "A water sprite. I have lived in this pond for hundreds of years."

"But how did you come to be here?" Kira asked.

The kappa bobbed its head from side to side but was careful not to spill the water in its bowl-shaped head. "The monks," it said, pointing its scaly, gnarled finger toward the mountains. "They brought me and my brethren here.

I claimed this pond as my own. It is smaller than the ones my brothers fought for. But it is all mine."

It slithered a little closer to Kira. "And what are you? Are you human or tiger? You have a tiger's eyes but a human body. It made me wonder which you would taste like. I like tiger flesh, but human flesh is so much sweeter."

"Too bad you'll never find out," Kira retorted.

The creature snarled and looked ready to attack when Jaewon came crashing through the woods, his sword drawn and ready.

"Kira! Are you all right?" he asked.

Catching sight of Kira in her underclothes, Jaewon flushed in shock and turned away, unaware of the danger right before him.

"Kim Jaewon! Watch out!" Kira yelled. But it was too late; the monster had changed course and jumped onto Jaewon, knocking his sword away and dragging him toward the pond.

Kira cut in front of the creature's path and stabbed at it. The kappa was remarkably fast. Letting go of Jaewon, it leaped out of the way, flailing at Kira with large webbed hands. Jaewon crawled toward his sword and yelped when the kappa ran over him. But no matter where it turned, Kira was there to block its path.

With a loud curse, the kappa tried to storm past Kira and jump into the pond. Anticipating its move, Kira side-stepped and caught it by its long hair. Water spilled out of its head, causing the kappa to visibly weaken. Realizing the water was its strength, Kira forced the kappa's head down, and then with one fluid move she impaled it through its back.

"Hundreds of years I've lived in my pond and you, tiger girl, have killed me," the kappa wailed. "Why didn't you let me go?"

"I was not about to let you kill for another hundred years," she replied.

"Curse you, tiger girl," it said. "Curse you a thousand times."

It gurgled, its body shaking in the grip of its death throes until it finally lay still.

Jaewon brought over Kira's jacket, holding it out for her to put on.

"What is it?" Jaewon asked.

"It is a kappa, a Yamato monster brought over by the monks. I've never seen anything like it. The kappa said that the monks brought over several of them, so we must beware of water now also."

Jaewon looked pale. "Perhaps we should stick to collecting dew."

Cleaning off her sword, Kira studied the kappa's dead body. "If we come across any other water sources on our way, I think we need to check them first," she said. "And clean them out."

The kappa was a terrible monster to let loose on an island population. If it was true that they'd been brought over by the monks, then Kira feared that the monks were truly as evil as she'd been warned.

6

Kira and Jaewon began heading inland again, toward the temple. After more than an hour of walking in the hot sun, they came across a large lake. Kira was keen to investigate it. As desperately as she wanted to find her cousin, it concerned her that the monks would have brought these creatures and left them in the waterways of the island. At the very least, she wanted to kill those kappas that she came across on her way to the temple. It also troubled her that daydreaming about whether Jaewon found her attractive had caused her to ignore her sense of danger. She was disturbed by how much of a distraction he was becoming. She had to keep her mind on track. Her one and only priority was rescuing Taejo, not flirting with Jaewon.

She placed her sword by her side and leaned over the edge of the water, seeking out the kappa. There was nothing visible in the murky waters. She splashed her hands in the lake, making a ruckus and trying to draw the kappa out. This time when she glanced down, she caught the unblinking glint of two large eyeballs moving closer. Pretending to stare off into space, Kira rested her hand on the hilt of her sword and waited.

With a rush of water, the kappa leaped out of the lake and embraced Kira's waiting form, only to be met by the thrust of her sword. Kira dragged the body away from the water's edge.

"This lake is a lot bigger. Do you think there's only one of them in there?" Jaewon said, staring in disgust at the kappa.

"I think so," she said. "I got the sense that they are very territorial."

As she was cleaning her sword, she suddenly heard barking, then the loud shrieks of what sounded like children. She put away her sword in a hurry.

"Damn!" she said as she looked all around them.

"What's the matter?"

"We are about to be discovered," Kira said, just as a pack of seven Jindo dogs crashed through the foliage. They barked happily and waved their tails, surrounding Kira as if she was their pack leader. Wet noses and tongues thrust themselves at her hands and face as the dogs were eager to show their approval.

"Down, dogs, down!" But still they pressed themselves on her until a shrill whistle called them to heel.

"I've never seen the dogs do that," a little girl's voice called out.

Kira looked up to see a group of children, ranging from six to ten years of age. Jaewon was staring at them with an expression of surprised pleasure. The boys were dressed in brown hemp jackets with white trousers, while the girls had on faded blue *hanboks* bunched up and tied about their hips, letting their long white cotton pants show. Many of them were holding water pails or big sticks. They were staring in shocked excitement, their gleeful whispers of "strangers" and "yellow eyes" filling the air. The little girl who had whistled stood in the lead. She looked to be about ten years old and met Kira's gaze with unabashed curiosity. She called out to the dogs, each by name, and yet they refused to leave Kira's side.

"Those dogs must really like you," Jaewon called out.

"You probably have food in your pocket or bag," the little girl replied.

Jaewon started laughing. "No, actually, I'm holding all the food in my bag. She doesn't have anything on her."

The little girl stamped her foot and slapped her hand to her thigh, calling to the dogs again. They whined, turned to her, and walked halfway before returning to

Kira's side. Kira continued to rub each dog's head affectionately, sending them into ecstasy.

Suddenly, the dogs noticed the body of the kappa and began to growl at it. The children all ran over to marvel at the creature.

"They killed the monster in the lake!"

"Our lake is free now!"

The children began to cheer loudly.

"Hey, mister, did you kill the monster?" one of the boys asked.

Jaewon shook his head. "She did," he said, pointing to Kira.

More oohs of delight as several of the kids with pails raced over to the lake to fill them up.

"How did you get water with the kappa in the lake?" Kira asked.

"We have a well in our village, but sometimes it runs dry or tastes too muddy," the first little girl said. "Then we come down to the lake in groups and half of us tease and bait the monster, while the other half get water."

"Weren't you ever scared?" Kira asked.

"As long as you aren't alone, it's pretty safe," the little girl said. "And the monster doesn't like noise or dogs."

Kira looked at them in approval. "You kids are smart."

"Who are you anyway?" the little girl asked.

"I am Kang Kira, from Hansong," Kira replied. "That big boy over there is Kim Jaewon from the Kaya kingdom. What's your name?"

"Lee Gina. Your hair is so short. Are you a girl or boy?" she continued.

"I'm a warrior," Kira answered with slow and deliberate intent.

"Your eyes are strange. Why are they yellow?"

"They let me see demons."

"What do demons look like?"

"Ugly. And they smell real bad."

"Kind of like Chul," one of the boys in the back yelled out.

The kids laughed, as the boy who must be Chul protested vehemently.

"Why are you here on Jindo?"

"I'm looking for my young cousin. He's on the island and I have to find him soon."

"How old is he?"

"Almost thirteen."

"Why's your hair so short?"

"I had to give it as an offering to the River God's daughters, in order to ride their underwater boat."

All the children oohed in delight. They clapped their hands and edged closer to Kira, causing her to step back in alarm. She was not used to the undivided attention of little children who seemed determined to touch her for some strange reason. She glared at Jaewon, who wasn't even trying to hide his amusement.

Gina suddenly smiled and ran forward, pushing both the kids and the dogs out of the way.

"Wow! You are awesome!" Gina said. Clutching Kira's hand, she started leading her away. "You must come to our village!"

Kira balked. "I don't think that's a good idea," she said. The children protested and tried to persuade them to come. They all began yelling louder and louder. The excitable dogs barked and howled in encouragement. The ruckus was becoming unbearable. She sent a beseeching look at Jaewon, who was grinning broadly at her predicament.

"Children! As much as we'd love to come to your village, we are trying to avoid being seen by the Yamato," he said. "It wouldn't be safe to go with you."

"But there are no Yamato in our village," Gina said. "They only stay in the coastal villages."

"That's not true," Kira said. "We came across a Yamato patrol about twenty li from here."

"Yes, but we are too close to the temple," Gina said. "The Yamato are really superstitious and scared of the Tiger's Nest monks. They won't come this far in."

At her words all the kids shivered, looking around them nervously.

"Gina, don't talk about them. What if they hear and come for us?" a little boy said, his voice frightened.

"I'm not afraid," Gina said, still casting a wary eye about her.

"Are the monks scary?" Kira asked.

One little boy came up close, tugging at her jacket.

"So scary," he said in a hushed voice. "They ride tigers and kidnap children and eat people!"

"They ride tigers?" Kira was surprised. "I wonder how they do that. I would love to ride a tiger."

"Didn't you hear the part about kidnapping and eating people?" Gina asked in exasperation.

"Oh yeah," Kira said, looking very serious. "That's definitely bad stuff."

The little boy tugged on her jacket again. "They've got tigers' teeth and claws and they hunt at night. They like to kidnap the naughty kids because they taste better. But first they shave off all their hair and fatten them up by making them eat only chicken anuses and grubs!"

"Hey, Chul likes eating chicken anuses! Maybe the monks will take him!" a boy yelled out, causing gales of laughter and angry cursing from Chul.

Kira bit the inside of her mouth, trying not to laugh.

"So you must come with us to our village," Gina interrupted. "It's not safe for you out here."

Jaewon turned to Kira and arched an eyebrow.

"Might as well go," he said. "It's not like they're going to keep us a secret. And maybe they can help. Besides, I bet they have rice."

With a heavy sigh, Kira acquiesced. He was right. The children were so excited to have met them that they would talk of nothing else to their elders. Any hope of sneaking by the village was now gone.

* * *

As Kira walked into the village, the first thing she noticed was an overwhelming warmth and sense of well-being. The market was crowded with farmers trading their wares; and men, women, and children filled the square with friendly chatter. Kira waited for the silence that usually descended when people caught sight of her. But it never happened. People pointed and stared with interest, but no fear, no disgust.

"Gina, who are these poor folk you're dragging through the market?" A heavyset woman with a smiling face stood up. She studied Kira and Jaewon with a smile that was perfunctory at best, her eyes sharp and appraising. She'd been sitting on a stool with a group of ladies who were all weaving a large fishing net spread out over the ground.

"Mother, this is Kang Kira from Hansong and Kim Jaewon from Kaya. The dogs found them! You should have seen how they went crazy for her!" Gina replied.

The woman took in the scene. The dogs pressed themselves against Kira's legs, their tails wagging furiously. Gina held on to one of Kira's hands while the younger girls held the other.

"I see that your guests are very popular," the woman said. She gave them another assessing glance and then smiled warmly. "Welcome to Haeyang village! We don't get many strangers here, but you are welcome to stay and maybe even trade with us. We are known for the strongest and luckiest fishing nets on the entire island!

Haeyang nets have been traded in Kudara and Kaya and even as far as Jinhan."

Gina broke in. "Mother, they aren't here to trade! They are on a very important mission."

The woman smiled down at her daughter and pinched her cheek. "All right then, Gina. Why don't you get our guests some food and make them comfortable."

With a bouncy thanks, Gina pulled Kira forward. When she looked back at Gina's mother, she was surprised to see her waving them off before sitting down and working on the net once again. Kira was shocked at Gina's mother's easy acceptance of them. Why was she so unfazed by Kira's appearance? What was it about these island folk that made them so free of fear? Why did their natural reserve change to a friendly welcome so quickly?

Gina and the children led them to a large building with an open, grass-covered courtyard with tables and low stools. Here, the dogs were chased away by an elderly woman with a broom.

"Ya! You kids get your dogs away from my food or I'll make dog stew out of them!"

Gina immediately ordered the other kids to take the dogs home while she brought Kira and Jaewon to a table. Once they were comfortable, the bossy little girl turned to the old lady and began to order food.

"And who's going to pay for all this?" the old lady groused.

Kira grabbed her money pouch and pulled out her

string of money. "We can pay for our meal, grandmother," she said.

The old woman looked in openmouthed surprise at her string of coins. Even Gina looked intrigued. She reached over and began fingering the coins in awe.

"And what am I supposed to do with that?" the old woman said. "I can't use that foreign stuff!"

"What is it?" Gina asked. "It's pretty!"

"It's money, coins," Kira said. "All of the Seven Kingdoms use them for trade."

"Not Jindo," the old lady said proudly. "Jade and gold pieces or barter. Maybe you have something worth trading for in there?" She poked at their bags, her curiosity intense.

"Grandmother!" Gina exclaimed. "My mother said for you to feed them. They don't need to pay. They're our guests!"

The old woman's sour expression lightened a bit. "Well, if the chief is handling the bill, then I'll provide them with an excellent meal."

Bowing happily, the woman toddled off to an open kitchen housed on the outside of the big structure. She started yelling at a woman minding the fire.

"Sorry about that," Gina said. "Grandma Song is known for being very stingy, but she is a great cook. Let me go get you some tea." She scampered off into the kitchen, avoiding the old woman's scolding.

"If she doesn't take money, then how can we repay

her? We don't want to be beholden to Gina's mother," Kira said.

"I'm sure we can hunt or do chores to help out," Jaewon said.

"But we don't have time to stay too long," Kira reminded him.

Sniffing the air hard, Jaewon grinned in euphoria. "Ah, but smell that food! I would gladly work hard for a bite of whatever she's cooking."

Gina returned with a small ceramic pot and teacups, catching Jaewon's comment. "But you don't have to work," she said. "My mom's the chief here, and you are our guests. Our guests don't pay."

"Thank you," Kira said. "We are very appreciative of your kindness."

"Then you can tell us a story," Gina said excitedly. "We never get any strangers in our village. Tell us all about the Seven Kingdoms and your cousin and the River God's daughters, and why they made you cut your hair!"

At that moment, the old woman came out carrying a large tray filled with food. Two bowls of piping-hot rice mixed with red beans and a large platter of grilled fish made up the main meal. An array of side dishes was also set out. Jaewon whistled in appreciation. Although the side dishes were simple, they hadn't seen this many since their last palace meal. Pickled cucumbers and cabbage; sweetened black beans; eggs boiled in soy sauce; tiny seasoned anchovies; and marinated watercress, seaweed, and beansprout salads. Kira's mouth started watering immediately.

"I will gladly tell stories all night long for this feast," Jaewon said in awe.

The little girl squirmed with joy at his pronouncement.

"This is an amazing meal. Thank you so much," Kira said to the old woman.

"The chief said to feed you, then I'll feed you! She's the reason our village is so prosperous," the woman replied.

"So the chief of your village is a woman?" Jaewon asked as he dug into his food. "I've never heard of that."

"Our clan has always had women leaders," Gina piped in. "My mother says that someday I will be clan leader. I already know everything that goes on in our village."

"That's because you're a busybody who doesn't know when to mind her own business," the old woman said.

"You shouldn't talk to your future clan leader like that!" Gina stood up and faced the grandmother with an assertive lift of her chin.

"Ya! I can say whatever I want to you, little girl. I'll be long gone before you get to put me in my place," the old woman cackled.

Gina deflated. "Oh, grandmother! I wish you wouldn't talk like that."

"Why? It's the truth. Nobody lives forever and that's a good thing."

"Yes, but nobody wants to be reminded of it all the

time, like you do," Gina complained.

Grandmother Song smirked. "That's one of the privileges of getting old, little one. I get to say what I want whenever I want and you have to respect me anyway."

Watching Gina interacting with the grandmother reminded Kira of Taejo. She had a sharp, painful awareness of his absence. She needed to keep going. She needed to find him before it was too late.

They ate the incredible meal quickly. Kira demolished three bowls of rice with red beans along with all the food served to them. She could have happily eaten the rice alone, she'd missed it so much. The simple meal was delicious.

By the time they finished eating, the other children had returned, bringing what appeared to be every child in the village. They sat in the grass, looking up at Kira and Jaewon expectantly.

"Tell us about demons!"

"What do they look like? What do they do?"

"Are you married?"

"How'd you get to Jindo?"

"How come you're wearing pants?

"Why is your face scarred?"

"Why are your eyes yellow?"

"Do your yellow eyes mean everything looks yellow to you?"

For a moment, Kira was lost in the memories of her childhood, surrounded by noble children taunting and bullying her. These were the same questions she'd heard all her life. And yet hearing them again from these children was a completely different experience. There was no malice or fear, merely curiosity.

She tried to get to them all, but each answer set off a series of more questions. Confused and dizzy from all the attention, she sent Jaewon a pleading glance.

Jaewon stood up and raised his hands for quiet. "Let me tell you our story."

At his words, the children erupted into excited chatter.

"I met Kang Kira because of a very special dog named Jindo," he said.

"That's the name of our island!" Gina exclaimed. "Why is he named Jindo?"

"Because that's where he came from," Jaewon said. "He traveled all the way up to the kingdom of Hansong, where he became the best friend of the crown prince."

The children became so elated at the idea of a prince having the same dog as they did that they burst into chatter once again.

"What does Jindo look like?"

"How old is he?"

Laughing, Jaewon shook his head at them. "I'm never going to get through this story if you keep interrupting."

They quieted immediately, staring up at him with bright expectant faces.

"It started with a *baduk* game," he said.

"What's baduk?" a little boy asked.

"Jung, shut up!" Gina yelled. "It's that boring black-and white-stone game that Grandfather Moon is always trying to challenge people to play."

Jaewon looked aggrieved to hear her describe his favorite game as boring but sighed and continued. "After winning a baduk game at an inn, I'd gone into the stables to check on my horse when I met a beautiful white dog named Jindo. Not long after, Kang Kira showed up and my life has not been the same ever since!"

The children all laughed at his dramatic pronouncement and Kira rolled her eyes. But it was a pleasure to see Jaewon interacting with the kids. He was a clear crowd-pleaser. She loved to hear him speak.

"When I left the inn, I never thought I'd see her again, but fate had other plans for us," he said. He explained how it was Jindo who found him and Seung and brought them back to help Kira when her party was being attacked by Yamato soldiers. The children banged on their legs and booed the Yamatos. They listened in rapt attention as he described the Dragon King's Temple hidden in the mountains and the prophecy. How the monks believed that the young prince was the Dragon Musado and how it was Kira's job to protect him always. The children all stared in deep admiration at Kira as Jaewon described her fighting abilities. Kira felt her face growing hot as he waxed poetical. She shot him an irritated glare until he continued. Then he told of how they took the prince north to his uncle for safekeeping and convinced King Eojin of Guru to bring the Iron Army and help fight for Hansong. Jaewon explained how some of the citizens began to believe King Eojin was the Dragon Musado.

The children gasped and one child got so upset he jumped to his feet shouting, "That's wrong! The prince is the Musado! Not the old king! They're all stupid!"

Such a loud ruckus ensued that Gina had to shout down the others for quiet so that Jaewon could continue. He described their secret trek down to the Diamond Mountains and how Kira and Taejo met the Heavenly Maidens, who explained where the first treasure would be. When Kira and Taejo went deep into the caves behind the Nine Dragons Waterfall, they found a large turtle who opened its jaws and on its black tongue rested a ruby as big as an apricot. This was the tidal stone that had the ability to control all the seas. He told them it was Kira who accepted the stone and Kira who wielded the power of the stone. And when enemy soldiers were about to kill him and his friends, she made an enormous water dragon out of the river that saved all of their lives.

This time Gina interrupted.

"It's her! She's the Dragon Musado, not the prince!" Gina shouted. "Am I right? I'm right, I know!"

Kira acknowledged her with a bow.

All the girls began to scream and clap in absolute glee. "I knew it! And she's a girl!" Gina was bouncing up and down in happiness.

Kira noticed that many villagers had quietly appeared, sitting down on the grassy area around them. They looked content to listen to the ongoing story.

Jaewon then took them through their reunion with the Iron Army and their return to Hansong. When he got to the part where Kira and the prince were captured by the traitorous Lord Shin, the children gasped in fear. They stared at Kira as if they believed she was in grave danger, even at that very moment. Kira pinched her nose to keep from laughing. She'd never been the subject of such adoration. The feeling was both embarrassing and uplifting.

"This part of the story might be scary for some of you young ones. I'm not sure if I should continue," Jaewon said sorrowfully.

A chorus of indignant complaints assaulted Jaewon. Even the adults began to yell at him. This time Kira laughed out loud. She loved the lively, playful interaction of the villagers. It was comfortable. It was homey.

"In Hansong, Kang Kira and Prince Taejo were trying to rescue the queen when they were captured by Lord Shin and the evil Shaman Ito. All three of them were marched through the streets of Hansong to face the firing squad on the cliffs overlooking the Han River. It was there that the beautiful queen saved her son and niece by wrapping her arms around Lord Shin's neck, throwing them both over the cliff. At this sacrifice, the citizens of Hansong revolted and attacked the Yamato, helping Kang

Kira and the prince escape into the crowds."

Some of the children and adults wept openly.

Jaewon went on to describe the exciting battle against the *imoogi,* where Kira used the tidal stone to create a water dragon that turned to ice. The ice dragon killed the imoogi and Hansong was saved. King Eojin marched into Hansong and proclaimed Prince Taejo his heir. The children all rose to their feet in thunderous applause. Even Kira had to clap in sheer admiration of Jaewon's storytelling skills. She couldn't take her eyes off him. He was magnificent.

Kira noticed that the courtyard was now filled with all the adults who had been in the marketplace earlier. They were listening as if spellbound. Someone handed Jaewon a ladle of cool water. He drank gratefully before continuing.

Next he told of the assassins that had infiltrated Hansong and killed King Eojin with cursed daggers from the Demon Lord. He described their escape from Hansong, to keep not only the prince safe but Kira as well. He described Whitehead Mountain and how Kira's and Taejo's spirits entered the land of shadows to search out the jeweled dagger. Then Jaewon turned to Kira to tell the rest of the tale. Reluctantly, Kira started to speak.

"In the land of shadows, we found the lair of Fulang, a very powerful dragon who wakes every hundred years to search out treasures and eat humans. He was to be the keeper of the jeweled dagger, which has the power to tear down mountains and cause earthquakes. But he had become greedy and he replaced one of his own claws with the dagger so that he could use its powers for his own covetous pleasures." Kira paused, unused to speaking before such a large and attentive crowd. This time it was the adults who yelled impatiently for the story to continue. It was on the tip of her tongue to tell them about Nara. But she was worried about their reaction to the idea that she had befriended a kumiho. Nara was too special to her. Kira decided to keep her role in the story private for now.

"I cut off the dagger from the dragon's claws and used it to escape. But I was stupid," she continued. "Without the jeweled dagger, I thought the dragon Fulang would be trapped forever. But I forgot his power and his magic. He tracked us from the underworld, shifting his cave so that it would open at the southern tip of Jinhan. He exploded out of the sand, took the prince hostage, and told me to come to the Tiger's Nest Temple in ten days. That's why we are here. To save my cousin."

The looks of fright and concern on everyone's faces told Kira what she already knew. The temple was dangerous. Gina jumped up and raced over to Kira, hugging her tightly.

"I don't want you to go there," she sobbed as tears flowed down her face. "Nobody ever returns from the temple. They're cannibals."

Kira rubbed a gentle hand through Gina's hair. "I know, but I have to try."

The children gathered around Kira in distress. Kira had never felt so much affection from strangers.

"If you find the prince, will you come back?" they asked.

"I don't know if I can," Kira said. "We need to return with all three treasures to where my brothers await me with the Iron Army. We must be ready to do battle."

"But aren't you afraid?" Gina asked.

"Yes. I'd be a fool not to be," Kira answered. "But sometimes we have to do things no matter how difficult or frightening they might be. Because it's the right thing to do."

A little girl, no older than four, tugged at Kira's arm. When Kira looked at her, she raised her arms, asking to be picked up. Kira's heart seemed to expand in her chest, making her catch her breath. She felt the tickle of tears in the back of her throat as she gathered the little girl into her arms.

"What's your name?" Kira asked.

"Miri," the little girl said shyly. "I like your hair. It's curly like mine."

"Thank you. I like yours," Kira responded, tugging at one of Miri's unruly curls.

Cuddling up against her, Miri asked, "Will you win?"

Kira couldn't resist holding the little girl tight.

"I'm going to do my best."

"Good," Miri said. "Then you'll win. I know it."

She leaned her head against Kira, perfectly content in

her arms. Her innocent trust and admiration reminded her of Taejo, causing a pang of worry to gnaw at her gut. Kira ran her hand over Miri's soft curly hair.

Gina pressed closer. "But after you win the war, you must come back. Please?" All the kids began a chorus of *please*, which made Kira laugh.

"I will definitely try," she said.

As the crowd began to disperse, Miri's parents came to take her home. Miri gave Kira a sticky kiss good-bye. Chief Lee waited for everyone to leave and then sent Gina home.

"Gina, why don't you go and prepare a place to sleep for our guests," she said.

"Yes, Mother," Gina said, running off in happy excitement. They heard her tell all her friends that the Dragon Musado would be sharing a room with her that night.

Once her daughter was out of ear range, Chief Lee sat down with a troubled expression.

"Do you have any idea what you will do once you get to the temple? How will you get in without being caught by the monks? How will you find the dragon and your prince? How will you escape?" the chief asked. "This way seems impossible."

"I have no choice," Kira said. "This is my fate."

The chief shook her head in pity. "You must pray to the heavens to have them send you a miracle. For you need all the help you can get. Their mountain is unnatural, but it was not always like this. Legend has it that there was a time when the monks were our friends and the temple was accessible to all. But then one day a young boy came from the mainland. He asked to become their disciple. They took him in and trained him, and he became like a trusted son. Unbeknownst to them, the boy's true intent was to steal the Dragon King's prized jade belt. He killed his mentor and broke into the heart of the mountain. But he was unaware that a dragon was guarding the belt."

She paused, looking at Kira with worry. "The dragon killed him. Overnight the temple mountain changed and warped into the unnatural creation it is now. No one sees the monks anymore, but boys and girls disappear every year. That's why the children must always travel with a dog. The dogs can sense the presence of a monk and warn the children to get to safety. It has been years since we've lost a child, but I hear the other villages have not been so lucky. People claim that the monks are cannibals, but I've never believed that." The chief shrugged. "It's ignorance. I think they take those children to become disciples. It's interesting me that the boys and girls taken were always the most adventurous and rambunctious ones. Never the meek or mild. The Tiger's Nest monks are warriors, first and foremost."

"That is good to know," Kira said. "It will relieve my friend's mind." Kira nudged Jaewon playfully. "At least you don't have to worry about them eating me," she teased.

Jaewon glared at her. "It's not funny. They are still deadly warriors and you are their number one enemy."

The chief sighed. "It's true. If you are here for the Dragon King's greatest treasure, then you are in grave danger. They will do anything to keep you from the jade belt."

The sun's fading light had brought shadows across the chief's face. With a bracing nod, she rose to her feet.

"Come, I will show you to your rooms," the chief said. She raised her hand to cut off Kira's protests. "It's too dangerous for you to travel at night. If it isn't the monks, it's the tigers that will get you. Better for you to leave early in the morning. You still have a half day's travel before you reach the temple. Rest here. I insist."

A sharp pain, like that of a knife slipped into her gut, brought Kira fully awake. Without lifting her head, she opened her eyes a crack and peered around the room. Gina slept soundly on a pallet next to her. There should have been no one else with them, but Kira knew someone was there. She felt it.

She turned to her side, freeing her legs of her blankets and reaching under her pallet, where she'd hidden her dagger. Now she faced the direction that she'd heard the intruder. Peering carefully through her lashes, Kira waited. Not long after, she saw the intruder approaching stealthily to her side. He had dark skin and wore only black trousers with a black sash tied around his waist. A long knife glinted in his right hand. As soon as the intruder got close, she lashed out high with her leg, catching him in the throat. With a quick move she jumped to her feet, hooking her leg around his foot and sending him crashing to the ground, facedown. She put her knee on his back and twisted his arm up, hearing the loud snap of the breaking bone. He dropped the knife, letting out an agonized cry.

Gina woke up with a scream, bringing Jaewon and Gina's parents running in from the other rooms. By then it was all over. Kira stood over the injured assassin.

Gina quickly lit a candle and ran to her parents.

"So you're a Tiger's Nest monk," Kira said. She studied him carefully. He was extremely well muscled and fit.

"I have to admit, I'm quite disappointed in your order. I didn't think you'd be the type to run to sneaky assassinations in the middle of the night. I thought you were honorable warrior monks."

His head whipped up in anger. "Come to the temple and prove your worth then, girl! Let us see if you are deserving of your title!"

"Prove my worth? To a bunch of assassins? You don't even know the meaning of a fair fight," she remarked.

His nostrils flared and his dark eyes narrowed in fury. "Who is not worthy? You, a proven thief, who comes to steal our greatest treasure? How should we treat you?"

"I come to save my cousin, who was kidnapped by

Fulang," Kira said. "If I am meant to have the third of the Dragon King's treasures, then it will come to me, regardless of what you might do to stop me. I no longer question my fate. I follow my path wherever it may take me, and right now it leads to your temple."

"Then come, Dragon Musado. I give you my word, there will be no further attacks from the monks until you enter our temple," he said. "If you make it, that is. Then you can show us your true worth."

She stared him down, judging the truth of his words before finally agreeing.

"I will be there," she said.

The monk rolled onto his feet, cradling his injured arm, and strode out the door into the dark night.

Kira followed him into the jungle, but he vanished out of sight. Even with her night vision, she was unable to catch any sign of the monk. Jaewon appeared at her side.

"I wanted to kill him," he hissed. "What's going to prevent them from trying again?"

"Pride," Kira said. "I think this was a test to see what I was like. Now they have some idea of how I fight. He'll report back to the others. They'll be ready for me."

"How did he get past the dogs?" Jaewon asked.

"Good question." Kira walked to the side of the house where the dogs were penned in. At first she thought the dogs were dead, so still did they lie. But then she heard the heavy snores and realized the dogs must have been fed a sleeping draft. "Well, at least he didn't kill them," she said.

Kira sensed Jaewon's nervousness and concern. She pushed him back toward the chief's house. "Come on, let's go get some sleep."

Inside the guest room, Kira found Gina waiting up for her.

"I'm sorry you were scared," she said. "Would you feel better sleeping with your parents?"

Gina shook her head, a smile bright on her face. "Are you kidding me? You are the most awesome warrior I've ever seen! I'm safer with you anyway," she replied. "I wish you would stay and teach me all of your moves."

Kira had to laugh at Gina's wild movements as she displayed her own fighting tactics.

"I'll tell you what—when the war is over, I will return and give you training tips," Kira said.

"You promise?" The little girl was beside herself with joy.

"I promise."

Kira and Jaewon departed early the next morning, laden down with food, leaving a tearful Gina behind.

"Don't forget, you promised to come back," she shouted, her voice breaking. "I'll be waiting for you."

Kira had a feeling Gina would still be standing there, waving, long after she could no longer see them.

The weather was warm yet breezy and the island

foliage was breathtaking. They walked in companionable silence for most of the morning, both lost in their thoughts. Jaewon was unusually quiet. He seemed stressed and worried about what was to come. Although she knew she should be concerned, Kira was still basking in the happy glow she had from spending so much time with the village children.

"I think you were a big hit there," Jaewon said.

"They were great," she said. "I'm going to miss them."

At home, she'd never spent much time around the little ones. She'd always been afraid that she'd scare them. But the other day had been an experience she'd always remember. Her heart felt full and tight and so happy. They hadn't been afraid of her. They'd liked her and admired her. The little girls had all told her that they wanted to be just like her when they grew up. She was unused to this type of affection. It reminded her of Nara and the friendship they had. It was a feeling she wanted to experience again and again.

"That Gina." Jaewon let out a small chuckle. "She really reminded me of my brother, Jaeho. So energetic and full of life."

Kira held her breath. Jaewon almost never mentioned his brother.

"I miss him so much," he said simply.

Kira reached out and touched his hand gently. He paused for a moment, his eyes sad but clear. "Jaeho was the most active kid in the whole village. Never sat still.

Bossy, but generous and caring. And he was so smart and popular. You would have liked him a lot."

"I know I would have," she said.

Jaewon started walking again. "And he would have loved you," he said. "Just like all those children at Haeyang village. You were their hero. I think you need to go back one day."

Kira felt the warm glow in her heart again. "I would love to."

It was midmorning when they heard the whimpers of a small animal. Kira was immediately on alert. She sensed that something was not right. Stopping in her tracks, she was assaulted by the acrid odor of otherworldly magic. It was compelling and powerful. Already, Jaewon seemed caught by its spell. He kept walking forward as if in a daze.

Kira gripped Jaewon by his sleeve. "We should avoid going in that direction," she said, trying to pull him away from the sound.

"There's something wrong up there," Jaewon said as he brushed her hands away and broke into a run.

"Wait!" She ran after him, alarmed as the odor intensified about them.

Up ahead they caught sight of an animal struggling—it was a tiny white Jindo puppy. It was caught in a hunter's snare and had gotten even more tangled in the ropes.

Jaewon pulled out his dagger, ready to cut the puppy free.

"Stop!" Kira shouted, as she saw what was under the

enchantment. "Kim Jaewon! Don't touch it!"

Jaewon ignored her.

Kira whipped out her bow and shot several arrows at the whimpering puppy.

Jaewon gasped and whirled around in fury. "How could you do that! It was a puppy! How can you be so heartless?"

Kira put away her bow and gestured at the body. "Look again."

He stared at her hard, his eyes accusing her of a devastating betrayal. It was as if he didn't know who she was.

"Turn around and see your puppy now!" Kira shouted.

He turned his head slowly, only to jump in shock. *"Ai ya!* How's that even possible?"

His face was ashen as he took in the sight of what was now a nest of dead mamushi pit vipers.

"That was a pretty strong illusion spell, but the magic never fools me," she said. "I can always see what its true nature is."

"But who did this?"

"The Tiger's Nest monks," Kira said. "You need to be more careful."

She collected her arrows and moved forward.

Jaewon came up next to her. "What kind of magic is it?" he asked.

"I'm not quite sure. I can sense shaman magic mixed with something that is akin to demon magic. But I can't recognize it," she said. "All I know is that it is powerful."

"You always were a very smart girl, Kang Kira," a sultry voice called out from behind them.

They both whirled around, their weapons at the ready, and were amazed to see the beautiful kumiho Nara leaning against a tree, languidly waving a delicate paper fan.

"Nara!" Kira cried out in joy. She slid her arrows and bow into their cases and ran toward the kumiho. Nara held out her hands and Kira grasped them tight. She was so happy to see her, she felt her face might crack open from smiling so wide.

"What are you doing here, my friend?" Kira asked.

Nara gave Kira's hands a tight squeeze and then embraced her. "Your thoughts of me were getting loud, so I was compelled to come and see you in person. I didn't understand how you could miss me so much when we'd only been apart for seven days."

"Has it only been that long?" Kira asked. "It felt so much longer."

"That's what happens when times are difficult," Nara said. "And I see that you are in a troubling situation already. I'm afraid I don't know the answer to your predicament."

Jaewon approached and bowed. Nara studied him intently. "I know who you are," she said. "You are Kim Jaewon and a good friend of Kira's."

Nara slid Kira an amused glance, her amber eyes glinting more gold than red. "And I have been very intrigued to see how close you two have been getting."

Kira's face burned with embarrassment. "Nara, you can see all my thoughts still?"

"Only those with the strongest emotions attached," she replied. Her eyes slid between the two of them, narrowing in amusement. Kira glanced at Jaewon, noticing how red he'd become when he realized what Nara meant.

Kira redirected the conversation. "Thank you for coming to help me. But you said you don't know the answer to our problem. Does that mean I am walking into a trap?"

Nara nodded. "Most assuredly. Fulang brought you here for only one purpose: to have you killed at the hands of the Tiger monks. He cares nothing for the prince. His sole desire is to retrieve the jeweled dagger. He will have warned the temple monks that you are coming for the jade belt."

Kira nodded and chewed on her lower lip as she surveyed their surroundings. "They sent an assassin to try and kill me while I slept," she said. "But when I accused him, he said I was to come to the temple and prove my worth."

"That explains why they aren't trying to ambush you," Nara said. "You must have proven yourself a strong opponent. For you have now been invited to their combat trials. You are apparently worthy enough to fight to the death."

This made Kira snort with unexpected laughter. "I

need to be worthy enough for them to kill me?"

Nara tilted her head. "This is no laughing matter. They will kill you anyway, but only the true Dragon Musado will actually be able to make it into their temple. They will deem it a great honor to kill you. It will be their three strongest and deadliest monks that you must face."

"*Aish!* We've gotta get out of here!" Jaewon began pacing back and forth.

Kira ignored him.

"And if I win?"

"If you win, you must get past two dragons—Fulang and the old dragon that guards the jade belt. And no one has ever survived the old dragon," Nara answered.

"For heaven's sake! Don't you have any faith in her?" Jaewon exploded. "Isn't there any scenario where she might actually win?"

"You seem to be under the impression that I would want this to happen to her. That is not the case at all. She is my one and only friend. I would not let anything harm her if it were in my power. I am giving her the facts of what might happen if she sets foot in the temple."

"So what is she supposed to do?" Jaewon asked.

"I don't know," Nara said. "I'm thinking."

"We don't have much time left," Jaewon said.

Nara stared at him with a calm, cold look and moved ahead.

Kira glared at Jaewon. "Stop antagonizing her—you aren't helping!"

Jaewon swiped his arm through a bush, sending a

flurry of leaves flying. "Well, she's not helping either."

"Give her a chance!"

Kira rushed after Nara.

"I'm sorry, he's really worried about me," she said.

Nara turned to look at Jaewon, who followed at a close distance.

"I know, which is why I won't bite him," she said with a wicked grin. "But he makes me quite hungry."

Kira shot a worried look at Jaewon. Not that she believed Nara would eat him, but it troubled her that her only two friends in the world were at odds with each other. It left her feeling distressed, right at the very moment she needed to focus on this most dangerous task before her. She hoped that they would try, for her sake, to work things out. Otherwise, she would have to leave them behind.

It was almost midday when they finally reached the valley of Tiger's Nest Mountain. Before them loomed the otherworldly vision of the mountain, with its high cliffs soaring toward the heavens. The obsidian cliffs reflected shimmering lights that gleamed like jewels set within the sinister walls. Nothing grew on the mountain. Its only purpose was to lift the temple up into the sky. The pristine white-and-gold architecture of the temple was set deep into the rock of its highest cliff, and there was no discernible way of climbing the mountain.

Gently sloping green mountains surrounded it, making it an incongruous sight—a raven set within a flock of sparrows.

"It doesn't look right," Jaewon said. "It looks completely out of place."

"That's because it's not real," Nara answered. "The monks built that mountain themselves with magic. It's not of this world."

"Are the monks even human?" Jaewon asked.

"Yes, but they have a magic that even I don't recognize," Nara said.

"The bigger question is whether or not that thing is even climbable," Jaewon said with an uneasy expression on his face.

But Kira was not listening. She was too busy assessing the face of the behemoth, analyzing where she should start climbing and what her trouble spots would be. No matter how long she looked at it, the mountain stumped her. It seemed impossible to climb. Only a bird could reach the temple. The enormity of the task before Kira left them all speechless.

It was the eighth day since Fulang's kidnapping of the prince and Gom. Kira was too close to fail now.

As they walked through the green valley, Nara halted. Her amber eyes rolled up into her head and down, then became vacant and turned inward. She became lost in a vision. "Wake the dragon and speak the truth," she whispered.

"Speak what truth?" Kira asked.

"Who is the true thief and who is the Musado," Nara answered. "At the highest point of the temple, combine the treasures and stab the dagger into the heart of the mountain. It will wake the dragon."

"But the dragon will try to kill me," Kira said.

"It is the only way," Nara said. Her eyes refocused and she blinked.

"What did I say?"

Kira quickly explained and let Nara think about her words.

"Then that is what you must do," she said.

"Wait a minute! The jade dagger's magic is the ability to cause earthquakes, right? So won't it bring down the mountain also?" Jaewon demanded.

"It is a possibility," Nara responded. "But it may be the only answer to the riddle she faces."

They were now close to the foot of the mountain.

"I can go no farther," Nara said. "Their magic is impenetrable. This is where I must wait while you complete your task. Your friend must stay also."

"What do you mean? I have to go with her!" Jaewon was furious at Nara.

"To survive this sheer cliff, she must concentrate on nothing but the climb."

"I will do it with her," he said.

"You will weaken her resolve and she will die," Nara responded. "I have foreseen this. You cannot make this climb, but she can. If you go with her, she will spend the whole time worrying about you. And when you fall, which you will, she will fall with you. But if you stay down here and help me, she might make it into the temple without getting killed."

Jaewon's face was a confused mix of anger and fear. He threw his bag on the ground, pacing angrily, and then turned to Kira.

"I would never do anything to hurt you," he said. "But the thought of letting you go in there by yourself fills my heart with despair."

Kira felt his panic. She leaned forward and held his hand. He clung to her, raising her hand to his cheek.

"If anything were to happen to you . . ."

She covered his lips with her free hand.

"I will return, and I will bring Taejo and Gom safely out of there," she said.

"You carry my heart with you, Kang Kira," he whispered.

"I promise to bring it back," she replied.

With a grim nod, he let her go.

"You must go now, Kira," Nara said.

Kira handed her bag and her bow and arrows to Jaewon, taking only her sword and water bag.

She took a step toward the base of the mountain, when Jaewon stopped her. He turned her around and gently cupped his hands around her face, kissing her. He tasted salty like the sea air and sweet like candied ginger. She closed her eyes and let the kiss overtake her until it was too much. Dragging her lips away, she put up a hand between them.

"You worry too much . . ."

"Be careful . . ."

Their words wound together as they pulled apart in self-conscious constraint.

"I love you, Kang Kira," he said.

"I know," Kira said. She turned away quickly, unable to look at Jaewon's face. Not wanting to see the disappointment that she always seemed to cause him.

Kira looked straight up at the mountain, assessing its obsidian surface. It was a little over three li tall. In order to get a better view, she walked a fair distance away to study the route up to the temple. The vertical rise was craggy with crack lines, overhangs, bulges, and ledges for the bottom third of the mountain. These petered out in the higher levels, where she took in the sheerness of the upper rock, with very few holds or ledges. She spotted some narrow ridges and a long crack through the heart of the mountain, but otherwise the upper half of the mountain looked virtually impossible to climb.

Without saying a word, she began to climb. Her sword and water bag were slung over her shoulders. As she anticipated, the first part was easy. She powered through it without breaking a sweat.

An hour had passed by the time she was a third of the way up the mountain and she had no choice but to slow down. The next reach would require a full-body swing to grab hold of a large crack. She hesitated, searching for a foothold under it. All she could see were a few small ridges that looked like they wouldn't hold her weight. But she had no choice.

Taking a deep breath, she swung her whole body over, reaching for the ledge. Her feet scrambled for the ridges, finding them and then losing hold as one crumbled, leaving her hanging on with one hand. She struggled to pull herself up and get a solid hold of the rock, wedging her feet against the side of the mountain as she pulled herself beyond the ledge.

She looked up at what appeared to be a straight glass-like surface. Desperate, she craned her neck to her left and spotted a narrow fissure more than her body's length away. She crawled crablike over the surface, crimping her fingertips over the smallest of edges in a mad rush to make it to the fissure. Squeezing her body into the narrow space, she rested her feet on a convenient crack and planted her back solidly against the wall.

Kira leaned her forehead against the inner wall and closed her eyes. She could feel the deep ache of every muscle in her body. The tips of her fingers were cracked and bleeding, and she wished she could get rid of her boots. Would she have a better grip with her toes? Looking at the mess her hands had become, she decided against it.

After a ten-minute rest, she began to crawl up the chimney-like cavity. It was an easy climb but ended too quickly. Popping out of the end of the fissure, Kira was faced with a short overhang. She propelled herself up to see where she was. It looked like the midpoint. But how was she to climb the rest of the way? Looking at her fingertips, she knew she had to be smarter. She was already losing feeling in them. This time when she found a crack in the granite, she pushed her hand in and clenched her fist, causing her muscles to expand and wedge into place. It was excruciatingly painful, but the tight fit ensured she wouldn't slip.

Higher and higher she climbed by sheer willpower. Blood seeped down her arms from the cuts and abrasions on her hands. She didn't stop, until finally she saw the base of the temple, three body lengths above her. It was so close. Euphoric, she reached for a hold, but the rock came apart in her hand, sending her falling, her body sliding down the face of the rock. There was no time to even scream as she desperately tried to catch hold of something. Anything.

Suddenly, her hands gripped onto a minuscule ledge, her body lurching to an abrupt halt as she clung to the face of the mountain. Kira let out a hysterical sob as she pressed her face against the cool stone, her heart pounding like a raging tiger within her chest. She swallowed down the bile that rose up her throat. It tasted of fear and rising panic. She didn't look down. She didn't want to see how close to death she'd been. Her hands were wet with sweat and blood and her arms shook uncontrollably. The whole front of her body had been scraped by the sharp edges of the obsidian surface. She could feel waves of pain rushing over her. She tried not to think of Nara and Jaewon below and how terrifying it must have been to watch her fall.

Kira didn't know how long she remained frozen against the mountain. Long minutes ticked by as she tried to get ahold of herself. Slowly she began to assess her situation. Spying a series of crevices to her left, she carefully repositioned herself into a safer spot. She dried her hands one by one on her jacket. The tip of her middle finger had been badly sliced by the face of the rock, but she couldn't stop to wrap it. She knew time was of the essence. She had to finish the climb before all her energy dried up. She lifted her body and jammed her fists into crevices left over right, toes wedging themselves into cracks. Her arms shook, her muscles were at their breaking point, but she kept climbing. Now her legs began to weaken, her thighs quivering with effort. But she wouldn't let herself fall again. Just the thought of it flooded her brain with sheer terror.

Then she saw a large crevice ahead, not quite in arms' reach, right below the base of the temple. This was it. She told herself that if she reached the crevice, she'd be safe. But there were no cracks, no holes for her hands or feet to slip into, only the smallest of bumps and ridges over the smooth surface. With one final effort, she crimped her fingers around any little surface she could and quickly scaled the wall with her feet until she grabbed hold of the ledge.

She clung to the ledge with both hands, just as her feet slipped with the mighty gust of an errant wind. She was flailing wildly, trying desperately to pull her body up with her weakened muscles. Against her will, she glanced down and felt her head spin. A fall from this height would be instant death.

Just let go.

She didn't recognize the voice that whispered in her brain.

Free yourself from the burdens of this life. Let go.

For a moment, Kira waivered under the temptation of release. No more pain. No more stress. No more being weighed down by responsibilities and self-sacrifice. She could be free of it all.

"Kang Kira!"

The sound of someone yelling her name jolted her out of her dangerous thoughts. It couldn't have been Jae-won. He was too far away. And yet she'd heard a man's voice just then. A voice that was vaguely familiar and yet unknown. It was a mystery she couldn't focus on. Instead, she concentrated on survival. Inch by inch, she raised herself until finally her head cleared the ledge. Swinging her leg up, she hooked a heel into the side of the crevice and pulled herself in.

As she crawled into the small cave, she thought she heard a distant shout.

"Kim Jaewon"—she laughed tiredly—"I made it."

The cave sat between the base of the temple floor and the mountain itself. It was only large enough for her to sit up in, but long enough for her to lie down fully. Every inch of her body hurt and her muscles were spasming uncontrollably.

She had no idea how much time had passed, but judging by the position of the setting sun, she guessed it had taken her over five hours to climb the mountain. She took off her sword and the water bag that hung over her side. The water was still cold and refreshing. Drinking deeply, Kira leaned against the cool rock and thanked the heavens for seeing her safely up the mountain.

"Taejo, I'm here. I'm coming for you," she said.

She poured the water over her hands, trying to get the worst of the grime off. They throbbed in excruciating pain. Lying down on the hard rock, she tucked her swollen hands under her cheek and fell into a deep sleep.

Blinking her eyes open, Kira was disoriented. She was in a dark cave. Slowly, she remembered where she was. Looking out of the crevice, she saw the evening sky as the last of the sun's rays disappeared over the horizon. She must have slept for an hour. She inspected her hands, unsurprised to find that they were completely healed. The fingertip she had nearly lost was now whole again. Her muscles no longer ached and she felt refreshed. Grateful to her tiger spirit, she prepared to enter the temple.

Pulling herself out of the crevice, she climbed sideways until she reached the end of the temple building. She scaled the rock alongside the temple wall until she came across an open terrace. Hoisting herself over the terrace wall, she dropped onto a marble floor and entered the temple.

It was empty. She wondered where the monks were. How was she to find Taejo and Gom? How did Fulang fly into the temple? Unless there was an open area at the top of the temple, Kira reasoned. Yes, she thought. She would head for the roof.

She entered a narrow passageway that flickered with candles burning in sconces. At the end was a small red door. She unlatched it and ducked her head to enter a spacious, windowless room that was empty but for the lanterns hanging from the ceiling. The walls were painted with a series of murals that depicted the battle between heaven and the underworld. Kira wondered exactly which side the monks belonged to. On both sides of the room were several racks filled with spears of many sizes.

At the other end there was a set of black double doors that were suddenly flung open to reveal the figure of a tall, muscular man holding a fearsome spear as long as his body. He was one of the largest men Kira had ever seen. His head was completely shaved and his handsome face was hard and angular and looked like it was chiseled from rock. He had hooded dark eyes under heavy brows that stared unblinkingly at her. Wearing only black trousers, his naked torso was smooth, bronzed, and hairless. Glorious muscles rippled with his every breath. He was an intimidating sight.

If the first of her tests was this monk, Kira was worried. He looked impossible to beat.

The doors slammed shut behind him. Kira bowed in greeting but the monk ignored her. He walked to a weapons rack and picked out a spear with a wicked tip. Turning to Kira, he threw her the weapon and beckoned her closer. Kira caught the spear in midair.

She studied him, watching as he settled into a strong stance, his rear foot planted firmly, as immovable as an oak tree. With his long arms and spear, his reach was far greater than hers. She would have to be quick or she'd be dead.

They circled each other, neither saying a word. She was not about to make the first move. She studied his movements, trying to learn his pacing and his breathing, anything that might give away his technique. He spun his spear slowly, trying to entice her to attack. Kira smirked. He clearly thought she was a beginner.

The monk probed his spear forward. Kira blocked the thrust by reversing her weapon and stepping into his low stab, binding it to the right. She tapped away several of his blows before making her first move. Parrying his downward thrust, she switched to a quick jab at the abdomen. He redirected it to the left side. Kira used the momentum to set up a high strike, just missing. Blocking another strike to her head, she feinted and was shocked when he almost struck her high in the chest. Barely able to parry it aside, the blade ripped through her sleeve, leaving a long cut across her upper arm.

In a desperate move, Kira slipped her spear in a one-handed parry using the base of the spear to try and extend her reach. Then she thrust it at his neck. His spear smashed hers out of her hand, sending it flying across the room. Kira leaped away from his attack and ran over to the rack, seizing another spear, this time one that was a little shorter and less heavy. Cold sweat pooled at the back of her neck.

"Flow like a river, Kira." She heard the whisper of her father's voice. These were his words when they were in training. *"Rock on your feet, balance is key. Don't be heavy-handed, be light. Think light. Watch your opponent. The spear will always betray him."*

This time, Kira matched her movements to the monk's. Watching carefully for the little cues of his body language to see where he would strike. She blocked and parried all his blows, seeing the rhythm with which he fought.

"Attack immediately, don't wait! Any commitment on your enemy's end is an opening on yours. Don't hesitate!"

The monk twirled his spear and tried to smash it on Kira's head. She blocked, parried, and rolled her spear, then went immediately on the offensive. On a high feint, Kira circled his spear with the tip of hers and separated it from his hand, stabbing at his jugular.

"Yield!"

The monk punched his hand down on the spear,

snapping the wood. Kira whipped the remainder of the staff around and smashed him on his head with the butt of her spear. With the recoil, she brought it around for an immediate side bash across his temple. He fell to his knees, stunned.

This was the opening she needed. One killing blow. But Kira couldn't bring herself to kill him. Although she knew he would not have hesitated, something stopped her from doing the same. Instead, she spun the broken spear high and slammed it down on his head again, knocking him out.

The black doors at the far end of the arena flew open.

Breathing hard, Kira wiped the sweat from her forehead. She picked up her sword and water bag and entered a hallway that led to a winding staircase. Holding on to the wooden railing, she began to climb. On the next landing, another hallway led to an open doorway.

She entered a large white chamber, big enough to hold a thousand people. It had several marble columns that rose into the high ceilings, painted to mimic a turbulent sky. The floor was made of highly polished marble as well. Her boots echoed loudly in the empty chamber. She took a long appraising look around her. At one end of the room there were double doors made of solid brass. At the other end there were large latticed windows covered with sheer red curtains that blew with a gentle wind. Thousands of candles flickered in numerous recesses in the walls that ran down each end of the chamber. Large lanterns mounted on ornate stands were positioned all about the room. In the far right corner was the small wooden door she had entered from.

As she turned, she analyzed the area, taking in all the details. Another room devoid of any furniture. The darkness of the painted ceiling, the brightness of the white room below it, were a striking contrast against the brass doors and bloodred curtains. Once she came full circle, she found herself staring at the seated figure of a warrior monk in meditation in front of the windows. The red curtains seemed to envelope him, surround him, caress him, as if they were his lovers.

He remained still; his hands rested casually on his knees, a glittering sword lay on the floor beside him. His head was not completely shaven, but his hair was cropped very close to his scalp. It was almost white in color, although he was not an old man. He too was shirtless, his skin a golden brown. He was all lean and sinewy muscles.

Kira stayed where she was and waited. She had no intention of approaching him.

A long moment later, he opened his eyes and Kira was mesmerized by their icy blue color, like the winter sky. Vivid and beautiful, but so very cold.

"So you are the Dragon Musado," he said. "I am surprised. I did not expect you to get past my brother. You have impressed us all."

"Where's my cousin? Where's Fulang? I don't have

time to waste," she said. "Tell me what you've done with them!"

The monk didn't respond, just studied her with an insolent gaze.

Kira could feel her temper rising. These monks were arrogant and rude. She would have spat on the floor but she wouldn't stoop to their level. Unwilling to waste any more time, she turned away and headed toward the brass doors.

A dagger sliced through the air, skimming her hair, and buried itself deep into the wall near Kira's head.

"You will not see your cousin unless you defeat the best of the temple monks," he said.

He rose to his feet in one fluid motion.

"I see you brought your sword," he continued. "Good. Let us begin our dance."

With a resigned sigh, Kira unsheathed her weapon.

Within minutes it was clear how good he was. He went immediately on the offensive, forcing Kira into a flurry of counterblows that sent her backtracking across the floor. The attack was nonstop; she had no time to think, no time to do anything but block and try to land her own killing blows. Already tired from her encounter with the spear monk, Kira knew she was in trouble. These monks were not fooling around. They wanted her dead.

"Use all your senses, little tiger."

Her father's voice whispered in her head. What did

it mean? Kira went on the offensive, sending several rapid-fire blows that he deflected with ease. She blocked and parried furiously, but could see she was boring him. Anger flamed within her, rushing her next strike. And then she felt the cut rip into her thigh. Blood was now dripping down into her boot. Feinting low, she lashed out with her right foot, tripping him.

In that moment her father's words suddenly made sense. She needed to use her strengths to give herself the upper hand.

As the monk rose smoothly back onto his feet, Kira raced about the room, cutting down the stands holding all six lanterns. She sliced off half of the red curtain and whipped it at the candles, extinguishing nearly all the flames on one side of the room. Using the fabric, she whipped it at the monk's feet, sending him flying. She then thrashed the curtain again, taking out the rest of the candles. The room was now in total darkness.

In the dark, her tiger eyes switched on and she advanced upon the monk. He heard her approach, fighting blindly. But now the advantage was with Kira. She approached with slow caution, knowing he would use his other senses. As she circled him, he whirled around, feeling her presence as she closed in. But in the darkness, his strike flew wide and he could not see the blow that disarmed him, sending his sword flying across the room.

"I can see your fiendish yellow eyes," he snarled.

From his belt, he took out a dagger and threw it at

her. She knocked it out of the air with her sword and mule-kicked him to the ground. She held the point of her sword to his neck.

"Go ahead and kill me, filthy Musado," he spat in his rage.

"I am done with you," she said.

At her words, the brass double doors opened, flooding light into the room again. She looked back and was shocked to find that the monk was gone. Quickly searching the room, she saw that he was nowhere to be seen. Kira froze, disturbed by the demonlike magic. It reminded her of the daimyo and his evil powers. This was magic that was not of this world.

Kira cut off a section of the red curtain and tied it over her leg to stop the bleeding. With a deep breath, she headed through the brass doors.

The third chamber was as vast as the others, reminding Kira of the unnatural magic that must have been used to create the temple. It was all white and well lit by numerous lanterns in every corner. At the very farthest corner of the room, she spotted a small wooden door. It called to her. She started toward it but halted abruptly.

Her challenger was already there, awaiting her in the center of the room. But this monk was female, with short hair and a sharp, intelligent face. She wore a sleeveless jacket that crisscrossed tightly across her chest and formfitting trousers. Thick leather-braided bands were tied to both of her wrists, but she held no weapons.

She studied Kira when she entered, her eyes filled with animosity.

The monk bowed and then moved into a fighter's stance. Her shoulders widened and the muscles in her arms stood out in sharp relief.

Kira returned the bow with caution. Her eyes darted about the room. Seeing no weapons anywhere, she prepared herself mentally to fight in hand-to-hand combat.

The first blow came out of nowhere. She hadn't even seen the monk move, but she felt the sudden kick to her chest. It sent her skidding across the floor. Rolling onto her feet, Kira took a second to catch her breath, her chest sore from the attack. Everything hurt. All the wounds on her body screamed with pain. The laceration from the spear on her arm and the gash on her leg both burned intensely.

The monk was now watching from the other side of the room, and a smirk played on her lips. Kira took a shaky breath, trying to control her pain. She kept her eyes trained on the monk the whole time.

One second she was across the room, and then a split second later she was right in front of Kira, letting loose a torrent of blows before Kira could make one move to defend herself. With a shrill shout of anger, Kira stepped into the attack and spun around viciously, striking the monk in the face. Before she could connect again, the monk disappeared. A moment later, she was leaning against the far wall, wiping away the blood from her mouth.

They reassessed each other. Kira tried to control her temper. The monk was using a type of magic similar to the one she'd seen Shaman Ito use on the cliffs of Hansong, right before she'd had to kill the imoogi, the deadly half-dragon, half-snake creature that had nearly destroyed the entire city.

"You need magic to defeat me?" Kira growled. "Not sure of your own abilities?"

The monk magicked herself in front of Kira again. This time Kira was ready. When the monk threw her first punch, Kira sidestepped it, raised her arm high, and bashed her knuckles into the top of the monk's fist. The monk shrieked. Kira savored the look of shock on her opponent's face. She knew from the blow that she'd broken the monk's hand. It hung limp and useless from the wrist. Before she could follow it with another blow, the monk vanished, reappearing on the other end of the room. Kira didn't wait, she charged forward. But the monk was nowhere to be seen.

Kira whipped around, seeking out her opponent, but she could find no one.

"Hiding?" Kira sneered. "Your magic can't protect you from broken bones, can it?"

Her gut twisted in warning and she whirled around. She was already too late. The monk had captured Kira by the neck, her nails digging into the pressure points. Crippling pain caused Kira's legs to buckle, sending her to her knees. She waved her other hand before Kira's face. It was no longer broken.

"Now you will know the true extent of my magic," the monk hissed. The monk pressed her fingers into Kira's temple, right above her scar. Kira felt a jolt of heat, like a lightning bolt, sear into her brain. It felt like her brain was going to explode.

And then Kira was in a vision, a memory of the past. She was in the Hansong palace throne room, lying on the floor. Her body writhed and shuddered in agony. She was Eojin and the cursed dagger was deep in her abdomen. The pain was so horrendous that Kira couldn't even scream. Was this the agony Eojin suffered in his last moments?

She had to stop it. Smashing her forehead into the monk's face, she broke the hold and staggered away. The pain vanished along with the vision.

Tears were streaming down her face as Kira stood trembling in horror.

"What are you?" she asked. "Are you a shaman?"

The monk was cradling her hand and her nose was spewing blood. She wiped the blood away, leaving a macabre mark. She spat blood on the white floor.

"I'm no dirty shaman," she replied. "But you have no idea what I am."

She vanished again and appeared directly behind Kira, her fingers pressed deep into Kira's temple.

Kira found herself back in the nightmare vision. This time she was beside her uncle Eojin, watching the cursed black plague creep up his body, trying desperately to control the curse and losing. The whispers of the Demon Lord amplified so that she could hear nothing else while the poison began to spread over her fingers and into her hands. There was no stopping it. She could only watch as it spread up her arms, over her shoulders, and into her neck. Kira opened her mouth to scream, but it caught in her throat as the curse marbleized her into a statue.

But just as she was certain death had finally come to her, the vision was severed. She was filled by the positive energy of her tiger spirit, as a golden glow emanated from within her. The monk was thrown across the room as Kira's tiger spirit leaped out of her and became a physical manifestation. Their golden auras were linked together. Kira sat up and put a shaky hand on her tiger's head and felt it solidifying into a real creature. This had never happened before. Her tiger spirit let out a roar that shook the foundations of the temple.

The monk fell to her knees, staring in disbelief.

"You are not the Dragon Musado! You are our VagDeva! Tiger goddess!" She prostrated herself. "Forgive me, oh merciful one! We were told you were our greatest enemy!"

Kira was shaking in agony and grief; all the pain and suffering of her uncle Eojin still clung to her nerves.

"VagDeva?" Kira asked incredulously. She pointed a shaky finger at the monk. "One moment you try to destroy me and in the next I must believe that you worship me?"

She shook her head. "No, I am not anything to you," she whispered. "I am the Dragon Musado."

Her tiger spirit growled in its throat and turned to lick Kira on her face. The large rough tongue rolled over her face, as if Kira were a tiger cub needing to be comforted. Her tears dried up and her sobs subsided as the pain soon faded away. All that was left was a sharp ache in her chest. She held her hand to her heart and rose to her feet. She saw the bright glow of her tiger's *ki* surrounding her. The warrior monk gasped in amazement and began to chant. All of a sudden, the entire room was filled with orange-robed monks, hundreds of them, prostrated on the floor in obeisance. As they chanted, they raised their arms to the heavens and bowed low enough to touch their noses to the floor, over and over again. Weaving their way through the bowing monks, the first two warrior monks approached. They threw themselves down at her feet, joining their voices with the others.

The drone of the chants filled her ears with a soothing hum, as she was embraced by the powerful magic that it bore. It was working together with the tiger spirit, bolstering its magic until Kira was completely healed.

She let out a deep breath, relieved to find the remnants of the Eojin vision gone. It reminded her of the pain her uncle was still suffering in the shadow world and of the vow she made to him. She promised that she would either free him or join him. For both of their sakes, she could not break her vow.

Facing the third warrior monk, Kira remained uneasy. "How did you do that? How did you make me feel my uncle's death?"

"My magic makes you relive the death of a family member and feel the actual pain they underwent," she said. "I am sorry to make you suffer so severely. I had no idea that the death you would relive would be so bad."

Kira shuddered. "It was my uncle's death. He was killed by a dagger cursed by the Demon Lord."

"That would explain why it was so brutal," the monk said. "My apologies, VagDeva."

"Why do you call me that?" Kira asked.

"We are the Tiger's Nest monks. We are followers of the tiger goddess VagDeva. She descended from the heavens on a flying tiger. You are her living reincarnation. The white tiger spirit lives inside you. We are honored to serve you," she said.

All the monks chanted "VagDeva!" and bowed to her.

With one last roar, her tiger spirit began to shimmer and vanish from view, leaving only the sparkle of golden light behind.

Kira stared out over the sea of orange before her. Could these monks truly believe she was their goddess? With her tiger spirit gone, the monks were quiet, staring at her expectantly. Kira closed her eyes. She could not be their VagDeva. This was not her fate. Not her responsibility.

Opening her eyes, she turned to the three warrior monks who now knelt before her, their heads bowed in respect.

"I have to find my cousin," Kira said. "Where is Fulang?"

All three warrior monks pointed at the small wooden door at the very farthest corner of the room.

"The dragon has deceived us," the female monk said. "He claimed you were a thief and not to be trusted."

"How do I defeat him?" Kira asked.

"We will help you!" the monk said eagerly. "We will destroy the blue dragon for you. We are yours to command!"

Kira shook her head. "I can't risk that. He might kill the prince. I must go alone. But I was told that I should wake the old one who guards the jade belt."

The monks looked at one another with great trepidation. "The old one has said that the next time he is awakened, the mountain will collapse," the female monk said. "But he would be strong enough to defeat Fulang. However, he may also kill you."

"If the mountain collapses, then the temple will be destroyed," Kira said, looking over all the monks. There were at least two hundred of them, now standing in front of her. They ranged from the very young to the very old. How could she destroy their home? What would they do without the temple mountain?

An old monk came forward and bowed deeply. "My lady, do not worry about us. You are both our VagDeva and the Dragon Musado. Only in our VagDeva would we entrust the care of the jade belt, and only to the Dragon Musado would the old one bear to part with it. You fulfill our purpose. There is no need for us to remain in this temple any longer. We will begin a new pilgrimage. But you must command us. What do you wish us to do?"

His words relieved her mind. She remembered that the mountain was unnatural. It would be good for the monks to start fresh.

"How do I summon the old dragon?" Kira asked.

"If you are the Dragon Musado, then you bear the tidal stone and the jeweled dagger. Hold both in your hands and strike the heart of the temple with the dagger. It will awaken him."

It was exactly as Nara had said. Kira spoke: "Then I urge you all to leave now and find a new home for your order. Go in peace."

The monks rose and chanted "Great VagDeva!" They all bowed in unison to her one last time before exiting the room. The only ones left were the three warrior monks she had fought.

"You must go with the others," Kira said.

"We want to help you," the sword master monk said, his head bowed down. "We must protect our lady."

Kira smiled. "Thank you, I appreciate your sentiment. But I must do this myself. It is my fate."

The three looked up at her, wonder in their eyes.

"You are truly our lady," the spear monk said. They bowed deeply.

Kira bowed in return. "And the three of you are the finest warriors I've ever fought. Go in peace."

With that, Kira headed for the wooden door. It led to a narrow stairway that spiraled up. She climbed for a long time, until she finally reached the top of the temple and walked out onto an open platform built into the side of the mountain. There were no walls except the mountain itself. Within the mountain, there was a small cave blocked by a metal barred door. She heard Gom grunting and squealing in greeting as soon as he saw her. Kira ran over to the door and peered into the cave. Taejo lay dozing in the corner.

"Taejo! Are you all right?"

"Noona!" Taejo's gaunt face looked painfully happy to see her. Both Taejo and Gom looked thin and hungry and were both grimy with dirt. Taejo was using his winter coat as a blanket. His blue silk pants were nearly black with dirt and his feet were bare. Gom's jacket and pants were filthy.

Kira held tightly to the thin hand that poked out between the bars of the door. The relief she felt to see him alive rushed into her head, making her feel dizzy.

"What happened to your boots?" she asked.

"They were too small," he said. "My feet hurt too much."

"I'll get you out of here. I promise," she said.

A low, insidious laugh echoed behind her. It gave her chills. She turned around slowly.

In the middle of the platform the blue dragon lay waiting.

"So you have finally come," Fulang said. "And you have fought your way through the tiger monks. You are an amazing human girl."

Kira didn't answer, watching the dragon warily.

"Well then, if you have made it this far, then you must truly be the Musado. Now give me my treasure and I will not kill the infant."

Taking the jeweled dagger out of her belt, Kira held it carefully in her right hand, close to the wall. "I will release my cousin and my dokkaebi first," she said.

Fulang let out a puff of steam. "I will burn you all to ashes if you disobey me," he thundered.

"I think not," she said. "Even you don't know what would happen to the treasure if you burned it." She smirked. "Otherwise you would have destroyed me the first chance you got."

Kira went to unbolt the cave door when a massive blue tail slammed inches from her face.

"Give me my treasure!" the dragon bellowed.

"You want it?" Kira yelled. "Here it is!"

She placed one hand over the ruby on her chest, then stabbed the dagger into the mountainside. Immediately the entire foundation of the temple began to tremble as the mountain itself cracked open. Deep within the recesses of the mountain, they heard an enormous bellow.

"What have you done, foolish human!" Fulang screamed. He swiped at Kira with his fearsome claws, but she ducked and scooted underneath as the walls of the temple exploded behind her. A massive silver dragon even larger than Fulang flew out of the walls and roared in anger.

"Who dares to steal my treasure!" His large gray eyes fell immediately upon Fulang as he let out a scream of rage. "You dare to show your thieving face here!"

The silver dragon attacked Fulang with great force.

As the dragons struggled against each other, Kira darted over to the prison cave and unbarred the door. Taejo ran into her arms while Gom bounded out and hugged her legs. The battling dragons crashed against the wall of the temple, causing the entire mountain to sway dangerously. They were going to destroy the temple.

"Brother, I beseech you! It is not I but that human girl who seeks to steal from you! She claims to be the Musado, but she has already stolen the jeweled dagger from me!"

The large dragon pinned Fulang to the ground and turned his great silver head to stare at Kira.

"Are you the Dragon Musado?" he asked.

Kira bowed. "Yes, I am! But I have not stolen anything. I come only for what my fate seeks to deliver to me." She pulled the jeweled dagger from the mountain wall and showed him the tidal stone in her hands.

The dragon stared down at the treasures in her hands and studied her face carefully. He then turned his head toward Fulang.

"You always were a liar," he said. The silver dragon bared his wicked teeth before biting Fulang's throat, mauling him until the blue dragon was still. Rising to his feet, the silver dragon threw Fulang's body down the hole from where he had come. The mountain began to crumble; the walls of the temple were falling in on themselves. The silver dragon grabbed Kira, Taejo, and Gom within his massive claws and flew out of the temple just as the mountain collapsed in a deafening clamor that reverberated throughout the valley.

He flew straight down to the ground and released them.

The silver dragon turned to Kira, bringing his great

head level with hers and examining her as if he'd never seen a human before. After a long moment, he drew back and closed his eyes. A sudden shimmering dazzled her eyes and then suddenly the dragon disappeared. In his place was a dignified old man with long white hair and a matching beard.

"It has been hundreds of years since I have taken human form," the old man said. He looked at his hands and touched his face. "I forgot how fragile it is."

"King Dang! The Dragon King," Kira gasped. She fell to her knees and bowed her head to the ground.

King Dang raised her up, holding her by the arms. He smiled kindly at her. "I've waited centuries for you to appear."

The dragon belt was around his waist. He unclasped it and gave it to Kira.

"Put it on, Musado," he said. "It is yours to guard now."

With trembling hands, Kira reached over to take hold of the treasure. It was made of fourteen white jade plaques strung together. From each plaque there hung a long gold chain of varying lengths, linked with precious jewels that ended in a miniature carving of a dragon. Fourteen dragons hung at the end of the chains, and each dragon was intricately carved out of gold, silver, jade, onyx, and other precious stones. Kira placed the belt around her hips and clasped it together. The shorter chains hung near the clasp with the longest one in the back, reaching to her midcalf.

She felt a sudden rush of power as the three treasures seemed to acknowledge one another. So strong was the sensation that it threatened to overwhelm her and she quickly unclasped the belt and held it in her hand.

The Dragon King watched her with great interest. From within his robe, he pulled out a small leather bag and a silver silk cloth.

"It may take some time to get used to," he said as he plucked the belt from her fingers. He carefully folded it up in the cloth and tucked it into the leather bag. When he was done, he handed the bag to Kira. He then turned to Taejo, who bowed with deep reverence. Even Gom lowered his head in respect.

"Little princeling, you are the heir to my throne," the Dragon King said. "But there will be many more trials ahead of you before you will receive my crown. You must prove yourself worthy. I will be watching."

The Dragon King took Taejo aside and began to talk with him quietly. Kira watched with Gom by her side. She didn't hear what was being said, but she noticed the sober expression on Taejo's face as he nodded in agreement. Looking down at the leather bag containing the last of the Dragon King's treasures, Kira gripped it tight before tucking it into her bust wrap.

It had been ten long days since his kidnapping, and Kira was amazed at the change that had come over Taejo. It was as if he had matured a few years during his captivity. He looked older, taller, stronger, and determined. She didn't know if these changes had occurred suddenly or if it was because Kira was finally looking at him with new eyes. When he finished talking with the Dragon King, he came over to her side and hugged her.

Kira looked at his bruised and dirty feet. "How long have your boots been hurting you?" she asked.

Taejo shrugged. "They were getting tight while we were up north, and then suddenly I just couldn't wear them anymore. But it's all right, Noona, I'm fine."

She studied him closely. "There's something different about you," she said.

He gave her a slight smile, his face exhausted but reserved. "I did a lot of thinking in there," he said. "I'm glad Gom was with me to keep me company."

He rubbed the little dokkaebi on the head. Gom grimaced and continued to hug Kira's leg.

Taejo's face was set, and the childish features had changed into something more mature. He was no longer a little boy.

"I'm ready to fulfill my destiny," he said. "I'm ready to be king."

In that moment, Kira had a vision of Taejo all grown up and wearing red ceremonial robes and the golden crown of Hansong. It was what would happen if they could defeat the Demon Lord. Kira was awestruck and euphoric. This was meant to be. Taejo looked majestic, the image of a great king. She had to smile as the adult Taejo was juxtaposed with the young one before her.

Then her vision disappeared.

"I'm ready for you to be my king," Kira said, her voice husky with pride.

In the distance, they heard Jaewon's frantic voice calling Kira's name.

"We're over here!" Kira shouted.

Jaewon came tearing out of the woods. He stopped short at the sight of them and then he charged forward. He threw down their bags before enfolding Kira in his arms. Gom gave an irritated grunt as he was dislodged from his hold on Kira's leg.

"The mountain collapsed and I thought you . . ." He choked on his words and hugged her hard. "You are always giving me a heart attack. I'm going to die young because of you."

Kira's heart was pounding in her chest. A hot flush crept up her neck and into her face at his nearness.

"I told you I'd return," she said gruffly. "But where's Nara?"

"When the mountain began to collapse, she told me to run for safety and then she disappeared," Jaewon said. "The last thing I heard her say was to look for you when the smoke cleared. I admit, I was only focused on you."

He rested his forehead against hers. "Thank the heavens you are safe."

"And my cousin too," she said.

She turned to look at Taejo, only to find her cousin staring in openmouthed surprise at them. Embarrassed, she pushed away from Jaewon, who was reluctant to let go until he too noticed their audience. Taejo was now grinning.

Jaewon smiled, bowed, and then patted Taejo heartily on the shoulder. "It's good to see you again, Your Highness."

"If you want to marry my cousin, I approve," Taejo said. "I know she really likes you a lot."

Kira hissed at her cousin, giving him an angry glare, but that didn't bother the young prince at all. Instead, he reached up and put his hand on Jaewon's shoulder, saying, "Don't worry about her brothers, I will make sure that they leave you alone. They have to listen to me, because I'm their future king."

Ignoring the two of them, smiling together in perfect harmony, Kira returned to the Dragon King.

"He is a fine man," King Dang said, a twinkle in his eyes. "You could do worse."

Kira gave an exasperated sigh. "I have a bit more pressing things on my mind right now, Your Majesty."

"Ah, but I disagree," he said. "Love is the most important reason. Why else are you here? You saved the young prince out of love, did you not?"

She nodded.

"Saving the world is a noble cause, but it is a grand gesture. We are true heroes when we act out of love," he said. "You aren't risking your life for the sake of humanity. You risk it for those you care about. There is no greater power in the world. And that is how you will save us all."

Kira looked at the old king with a troubled expression. "But love is also our greatest danger, isn't it? When we are willing to risk all for love, it also means we sacrifice ourselves for others. I don't want anyone sacrificing themselves for me anymore."

Images of her father's and her aunt's sacrifices swept through her mind.

King Dang took hold of her hands. "My dear girl, if you were in a position to save someone you loved by sacrificing yourself, would you do it?"

"Yes," she said. "Of course."

"Then how can you stop someone from doing the same for you? Would you take away their freedom?"

"No, of course not, but you miss my point," she said.

He held up a hand, stopping her words. "I think I do understand you," he said. "You do not believe you are worth anyone's sacrifice."

Kira's lips snapped shut.

"Young one, you must trust in your own self-worth. You must love yourself and respect who you are," he said. "Only then will you recognize your true value—that which lies in the heart of you."

It wasn't that Kira hated herself or devalued her own worth. Perhaps it was more accurate to say that she valued others more than she valued herself.

She heaved a sigh. "I know my worth," she said.

"Do you really?" he asked. "For I fear that there will

be more danger and heartache ahead for you. And you must stay strong, no matter how difficult it proves to be. No matter how beaten down you feel, you must not give up. Rely on your strengths and have faith in yourself. No one else can do that but you."

He was silent as he stared gravely at her, his eyes sorrowful. "I wish I could keep you from the suffering that you will endure. But I have faith in you, Musado. If only you will have faith in yourself."

"I will try my best," she said.

"That is all I can hope for," he answered. "Now let us go someplace safe where the prince can rest for the night."

The Dragon King led them farther into the forest, where they came upon an ancient shrine.

"We will rest here for the night," said the Dragon King. "Tomorrow I shall fly you to the mainland."

Kira heard Jaewon whisper to Taejo in confusion, "How is he going to fly us anywhere?"

Inside, the shrine was old, dusty, and covered with cobwebs. With a clap of King Dang's hands, the shrine instantly shimmered into its original beauty. The gold statues sparkled and candles lit the room in brilliance. At the far end of the shrine, there was a large table surrounded with luxurious cushions.

"Come, sit," the Dragon King said. "You must be hungry."

They sat on plush cushions on the carpeted floor and watched as plates and utensils appeared on the table. On each plate was a small, steaming-hot white towel. Taejo unraveled it quickly and wiped down his hands, face, and neck. By the time he was done, the towel was black with dirt. Kira wiped her hands, enjoying the heat. Gom didn't want to touch his, but reluctantly acquiesced at Kira's insistence. She wiped the little dokkaebi's face and hands off, using both her towel and Gom's to get the worst of the dirt off.

"You might as well give up," Jaewon whispered. "The only way he'll get clean is a bath. A long hot bath!"

King Dang clapped his hands twice and unseen hands brought out platters of food, fruit, and drink. The aroma was tantalizing. What looked like an entire roasted pig drifted by Kira's nose, causing her mouth to instantly salivate. Beautiful, thinly sliced layers of raw fish were laid over slivers of cucumbers. Hot pots, still bubbling with spicy stews, and noodle dishes mixed with beef and vegetables landed right in front of Kira. Seasoned bean sprouts, marinated spinach, vinegary pieces of julienned radish, and pickled cabbage surrounded the main dishes.

Gom grunted happily when several large meaty bones appeared on his plate.

Kira watched as Taejo dived into a stewed chicken dish that was fragrant with ginseng and ginger.

"Take it easy," Kira said to him. "Has it been a while since you've eaten? You don't want to upset your stomach."

Finishing off his bite, Taejo breathed a sigh of contentment. "Fulang only let the monks come up once a day.

It was just one meal and I had to share it with Gom. It was never enough for both of us."

With that pronouncement, he dived back into his food. Before Kira could admonish him again, another platter filled with braised short ribs, potatoes, radishes, and carrots was placed in front of her. Spotting the potatoes, Kira's eyes lit up. She remembered how much Jaewon loved them. Spearing several potatoes with her silver chopsticks, Kira placed them on Jaewon's plate. His gleeful expression made her laugh as he downed them in two bites. She placed more potatoes on his plate along with a hefty serving of the short ribs and then served herself.

The first bite of the short ribs melted in her mouth and caused Kira to close her eyes in rapture. This was the best food she'd ever eaten in her entire life.

"Your Majesty, this is delicious," Kira exclaimed. Jaewon and Taejo nodded, with mouths too full to speak. Gom was happily gnawing on his bones.

The Dragon King smiled, eating his food with elegant refinement. "It's been so long since I've had a good meal," he said. "I'd forgotten how good human food is."

"Were you asleep in your dragon form this entire time?" Kira asked.

The king nodded. "The Heavenly Father asked me if I was ready to return home, but I was too troubled. I knew I could not rest easy with the prophecy heavy on my mind. So he gave me the choice to stay and guard the belt. To keep it out of the wrong hands and pass it only to the Musado. I have slept for centuries, undisturbed except for one unfortunate incident. Now that my job is done, I can alight to the heavens."

"But why can't you stay here and help us?" Kira asked.

He continued to eat for several minutes without answering. Kira began to wonder if she'd offended him when he finally put down his chopsticks, took a drink of plum wine, and answered.

"It is not that I don't want to help, but it is that I cannot," he said, a sympathetic gleam in his wise old eyes.

"This is no longer my fight. It is yours. This is no longer my destiny but his," he said, pointing at Taejo. "I did all that I could to protect the human world. Now it is your turn."

"But what if we fail?" she asked.

"I don't know," he said. "But to think of failing before we have even begun is to set yourself up for failure. Do not forget that you have something that the Demon Lord does not understand."

"What is that?" she asked.

"The capacity to hope," he replied. "It is a singularly human emotion and comes out of a human's ability to believe in things, in destiny, and in one another. If you never give up hope, you will not fail."

"Hope is one thing I have a lot of," Kira said.

King Dang looked approvingly at her. "That is why you are my Musado."

Soon Taejo was falling asleep where he sat and even

Gom had curled up into a ball around his gnawed-over bones. Jaewon helped Taejo out of the shrine and Kira picked up her little dokkaebi, marveling at how light he was. Even fast asleep, Gom kept a tight grip on his cudgel.

The old king led them to a small hut nearby that looked too small to house them all, but when they entered, they found that the house was actually part of the mountain it was built into. Taking off their shoes, they wandered into the house and were surprised to see it extended into numerous chambers, all with comfortable sleeping pallets, blankets, and pillows. There was even a bathing room in the rear of the building. It was where the hot spring waters ran out of the cave and poured into a large wading pool. Kira was eager to try it.

Jaewon guided Taejo into an empty room and tucked him into a bed. As Jaewon covered her cousin with a blanket, she watched as his hand reached out, as if searching for something. Kira laid the little dokkaebi next to him. He made a little grunting sound and curled up by Taejo's side. Taejo was sound asleep.

"Thank you, Gom," Kira whispered.

They stepped out and thanked the Dragon King for all of his help.

"The prince needs more rest and emotional comfort," the Dragon King said. "Tomorrow I will take you someplace safe."

He left them to find their own ways to their rooms.

Jaewon followed her and stood at her door.

"I died a thousand deaths watching you climb that mountain," he said.

Kira paused and looked at him with sympathy. "I know," she said. "It was hard for me too."

He let out a soft chuckle. "*Hard* is such an insignificant word," he said. "Nara was right. I would never have been able to climb it with you. I would have been a burden."

Kira got to her feet and walked over to him. "It was good that you didn't come. I don't know what I would have done if anything had happened to you."

They stood smiling at each other, the moment tense with the strong emotions that they had both felt that day. He leaned forward but Kira pulled away.

"I'm going to go clean up," she said.

"I guess I have to sleep in my own room tonight," he said with a sigh.

Kira gave him a pointed look.

"I know, I know," he said. "But I'm going to miss sleeping next to you. I'll even miss your snoring."

Walking by him, she gave him a playful push. "I don't snore," she said, heading to the bathing room.

"Yes, you do," he replied. "Most of the time it's cute and soft. But sometimes you snore like a bear."

He followed her to the door of the bathing room, where Kira stood blocking the way. "Well, it's a good thing you have your own room tonight, then," she said.

"Now you can sleep undisturbed."

She shut the door in his face and prepared for her bath.

"But now I can't sleep without it," he said plaintively at the door.

"Too bad," Kira said. "Now go away."

He was quiet for a moment and then knocked on the door again.

"Go away, Kim Jaewon!" she said.

He kept knocking. With an aggravated huff, she slid the door open to yell at him and was surprised when he cupped her face in his hands and kissed her.

"I'm so glad you made it safely," he said. "Good night."

With a bow, he slipped away.

Kira shut the door with a smile. After a refreshing bath in the hot springs that washed away her grime and rejuvenated her spirit, Kira changed into her clean set of clothes, washed out her dirty ones, and settled in for the night. She was clean, full, and for once she felt completely safe.

11

In the morning, Kira made both Taejo and Gom bathe. Taejo complained that without clean clothing to change into, it was all a waste of time. But when they were finished, he was surprised to find his old clothing was gone. A clean new blue silk outfit and a brand-new pair of boots were waiting for him. Even the little dokkaebi had new brown shirt and pants to wear.

"Not such a waste of time, huh?" Kira said. "And you both smell much better."

Kira and Jaewon packed up their bags, surprised to find that everything they owned had been cleaned.

"Don't get me wrong," Jaewon said. "I'm very grateful.

But where are they? Are they watching us all the time? It's a little creepy."

He looked around as if expecting ghosts to pop out of the walls.

"You're so dramatic," Kira said, shaking her head. "I doubt they're hanging around spying on us. It's not like we're that interesting."

"I can't believe you don't think it's weird," he huffed. He turned to Taejo. "Don't you think it's weird?"

Taejo shrugged.

"Ah, nobles," Jaewon said. "You're used to having servants underfoot all the time. I guess invisible ones are no different."

All packed up and ready to go, they entered the shrine. The banquet table was once again filled with delicious food for them to eat for their morning meal, but the Dragon King was not there. There were only three table settings and the unseen hands seemed anxious to feed them. Plates floated quickly back and forth across the table and vanished as soon as they served themselves from it. After they ate, they heard a loud rustling sound outside.

"That must be King Dang," Kira said.

They exited the shrine and found the great silver dragon waiting for them at the door. His beautiful silver scales glinted in the sunlight like thousands of sparkling diamonds.

"That's the Dragon King?" Jaewon marveled.

The dragon turned to look at them and inclined his head in a stately nod. Then he gazed directly at Kira.

Come, Dragon Musado, climb onto my back. I will take you all to where you must go.

His voice spoke directly into her mind. With a nod, she urged the others onto the dragon and climbed up front. The dragon took off into the air, undulating through the skies in a slow but steady pace. Little Gom wrapped his arms around Kira's waist and squeaked in alarm. Kira let out a crow of laughter and flung out her arms. This was even better than riding the *chollima*. There were no wings that threatened to knock you off, only the smooth rolling sensation of floating in the clouds. It was magical.

She looked down, hoping to see Haeyang, Gina's village. But they were already too far up in the sky to see.

Not even an hour had passed when the dragon began to descend from the skies. He was heading into a mountain range, green and filled with the vibrant colors of spring. To the south, Kira spotted acres of tea bushes. She wondered if these were the famous tea farms of Kaya that Seung had once talked about so proudly.

They descended lower into a valley hidden by a deep forest.

I believe this is the right place for you, he said. *I sense the presence of someone close to you.*

"My brothers?" Kira asked hopefully.

Not your brothers, but someone who has been praying for you and the prince. You will be safe now.

"Sunim," she said. "You have heard his prayers?"

Yes, he is my disciple. He will be coming shortly.

"But he was so far north? How can that be?" Kira marveled.

You must ask him yourself.

Somehow the dragon navigated into a small clearing and landed gently. Kira climbed down and stood before the dragon.

"Thank you, Your Majesty, for everything," she said. Taejo and Jaewon bowed deeply and reiterated their thanks.

The dragon inclined his head.

Musado, I must warn you. The belt is not to be used if one can help it. It is a powerful weapon. Too powerful. While only the Dragon Musado can use it, even the true Musado may not be able to wield its power effectively. For once the dragons are released, they will wage a destructive force more powerful than that which you wish to battle.

Kira was shaken. "Why did I not know this? It would have been better in the temple, then."

No, I was only ever the guardian. For this prophecy to come true, all the treasures must be together.

"Then I must never use it."

I hoped you would say that, the dragon replied gravely. *But the greater danger lies in you.*

"What do you mean?"

If you are captured and your mind is controlled by the Demon Lord, he may force you to release the dragons.

"I won't let that happen." Kira's reply was fierce. She

felt a rush of anger as she realized that she might be the end of their world. All the treasures were not a protection. They were an absolute danger. For a moment, she wanted to scream, to release all her anger, frustration, and worry. It just wasn't fair.

The dragon nudged her. *You must stay strong of mind, child, for you will need it.*

The dragon lifted his head and stared off into the darkness. *Someone approaches. I must leave you now.*

He touched his muzzle to Kira's cheek and then leaped straight into the air, his long body undulating through the azure sky. Kira wished she could fly away with him and leave all her worries behind.

They heard the barking of a dog that was immediately recognizable.

"Jindo!" Taejo shouted and began to run toward the now visible white form. Far behind, Kira spotted the forms of Brother Woojin, Seung, and Major Pak.

"I don't believe it! How can they possibly have gotten here so quickly?" she asked.

Jindo had reached Taejo's side and was having an ecstatic reunion with his master. It brought tears to Kira's eyes to see how happy the two of them were.

Wiping away her tears, she looked around. "I wonder where we are."

"We are right near Flower Hill Temple at Mount Jiri, in Kaya," Jaewon said, his voice sounding hoarse. "We are near my hometown."

"Is this the temple where your . . ." Kira's voice trailed off, unable to finish her question after seeing the pain on Jaewon's face. It was not easy for him to be so close to home and remember his brother's death.

"No, not this one. Our village went to Stone Mountain Path Temple. It is on the other side of the mountain. That's where he died," he said. He let out a harsh breath. "I don't think I could go there."

She placed a comforting hand on his arm. "There's no reason for us to go," she said. "Come, let's go meet the others and find out how they got here."

They walked to where the others were greeting Taejo, his faithful dog pressed tight to his side. At Kira's approach, Jindo barked in greeting and jumped up to lick her face. Gom growled in disapproval but then was subjected to a thorough licking by the dog. Grunting, the little dokkaebi hid behind Kira, trying to avoid the curious dog.

Jaewon reached over and pulled Seung into a bear hug and pounded him on his shoulder.

"It's good to see you again," he said. "It's amazing how much I missed your big mouth while you were gone."

"I think you meant my cooking, for I know how bad yours is," Seung said.

Jaewon sputtered indignantly. "That's not true at all! I'll have you know I made a seafood stew that even Kang Kira raved over!"

"She must have been really hungry," Seung retorted.

The two friends grinned at each other as Brother Woojin and Major Pak greeted Kira warmly.

"Are you all better?" she asked Major Pak, examining him thoroughly.

"I had the best caretaker," he replied, pointing at Seung. "I'm in perfect health."

"I'm so relieved to hear that. But I did not think I would see you for many weeks! What magic made this possible?" she asked.

"The most beautiful sight that I have ever seen descended on us at North Wagay," Brother Woojin rhapsodized. "Several chollimas flew into the village. They made quite a miraculous display before they were able to communicate with Shaman Won. He told us that they'd been sent by the Dragon King, who commanded them to bring us to Flower Hill Temple. We arrived late last night and then, less than an hour ago, I heard the voice of the Dragon King giving me word that you were coming."

Then Kira understood. "He told me he was finding a safe place for Taejo."

"Shaman Won also said that the rest of your dokkaebi army is heading down to meet you. Because they don't need to rest and are very fast, they should come find you within two weeks," Brother Woojin said. "In the meantime, we will rest here. I have sent a few messengers to your brother and the Iron Army to let them know where we are."

Kira agreed, relieved to hear that her brothers and

the dokkaebis were on their way.

"But let us return to the temple. I can see the prince has been through a terrible ordeal," Brother Woojin said.

Looking over at the prince on the grass, hugging his dog, Kira saw the exhaustion on his gaunt face. Anger at Fulang flooded her.

She went over to her cousin and helped him up to his feet. "Come on, let's go find you some more food," she said. She squeezed his arms, noting how thin he'd gotten. "We need to get your strength back again."

Taejo smiled at her. "You don't have to worry so much," he said. "I'm not a child anymore. I can take care of myself."

It was not only physically that Taejo had matured but emotionally as well. Even his voice had taken on a deeper and more serious intonation. His words were calm and gentle, but Kira caught the strength of character behind them.

"You're right," she agreed with a deep bow. "You're not a child anymore. You are our king."

12

Pink arrowroot flowers bloomed in splendor all around the temple grounds. It was easy to see how the temple got its name. The blooms were so thick that a person could lie down comfortably in a bed of fragrant flowers without ever touching the ground.

The monastery had been abandoned by the monks when they'd heard the news of the Yamato invasion. Only a few caretakers had remained behind. But the grounds were untouched by any evil. Kira hoped that the monks would return someday soon, for the temple was too beautiful to remain empty.

The grounds included a monastery and a guesthouse.

Taejo and the other men were all housed in the monastery, while Kira stayed in a small room in the guesthouse. Brother Woojin had insisted on keeping Kira separate from the men for her privacy. With Major Pak and Jaewon rooming right next to Taejo, Kira was able to enjoy her time alone. The temple filled her with a peaceful tranquility that was a balm to her tired spirit. She also had much to think about, given her conversations with the Dragon King. Ever since his admonition about the jade belt, it had felt like a boulder sitting on her chest. A physical manifestation of all the stress and worry she was feeling. It was a treasure she would have felt better never having. She knew that one misstep on her part might destroy everything. The little leather bag tucked into her bust wrap was a constant, uncomfortable reminder of the danger that they all faced.

Kira stood in a clearing between the temple's guesthouse and the forest, practicing her early morning *taekkyon* exercises. She breathed in the cool, crisp mountain air, expelling it with every fluid movement of her body.

She heard her father's voice in her head, admonishing her to keep her form controlled yet elegant, strong yet beautiful.

"How you fight in combat and how you practice forms are two very different things. The first is self-defense, but the second is art. It is your connection between mind and body."

Every move, every subtle detail of her taekkyon

forms, were a mastery of grace and strength. Her father had seen to that. Each punch and kick, every pivot and jump, had been done thousands of times before. They were an artistry of motion and timing and control.

She remembered when she was five years old her father had taken her to see the *saulabi* practicing their taekkyon forms. As they watched the perfect choreography of the soldiers in motion, her father had said, "There's no dance as perfect as this one."

When she practiced, it was in homage to him.

"Good morning, young mistress!" Brother Woojin called to her as he approached with Jaewon.

Kira relaxed her stance and bowed. "Good morning, Sunim."

"What a beautiful day for your birthday!" Brother Woojin said. "We will have a lovely celebration for you today!"

"My birthday," Kira said in surprise. "I almost forgot."

It was the twentieth day of the fourth month of the solar calendar.

"Yes, it's a good thing Sunim remembered. Seung has made the most delicious seaweed soup for your birthday breakfast," Jaewon said.

Thinking of her birthday brought a wave of homesickness and a longing for her parents. Like everyone else of the Seven Kingdoms, Kira counted her age by the passing of each new lunar year. But her birthday was the day to celebrate her mother's labor of love. Eighteen years ago today, her mother had given birth to her. Every year, her mother would tell her how much she looked forward to Kira's birthday because it brought the flowers and warm weather and her favorite day. The day she was gifted with a daughter. It would be Kira's first birthday without her mother.

The smile slipped from her face. Unwilling to let the others see the tears that threatened to spill over, Kira turned abruptly and walked away.

She found herself in a lotus pond garden. Stone stupas and statues artfully decorated the peaceful garden. She sat on a low bench in front of a pond filled with vividly colored carp that poked their heads out in hopes of food. It reminded her of the queen's fragrant pavilion and of feeding the fish on the bridge with her mother. She held back the tears that threatened to overcome her. She didn't want to cry. She wanted to think of her mother without tears. There was nothing she could do about the aching in her heart, but she wanted to remember all the happy times with her mother.

On her tenth birthday, she and her mother had sneaked into the kitchen and chased away the servants. They'd made meat dumplings and fried rice and finished it all off with sweet rice cakes filled with delicious red bean paste. She remembered laughing with her mother at her own pathetic dumplings. Kira had filled her dumplings with too much meat and the wrappers had fallen apart. Kira had eaten her mother's perfect crescent-shaped dumplings while her mother claimed to enjoy Kira's misshapen ones.

"Why are you eating the bad ones, Mother?" Kira asked.

"These are not bad at all! These are the best dumplings in the world, because my darling daughter made them for me. Even your father would agree with me."

"But not my brothers." Kira giggled.

"Yes, even them!" Her mother laughed with her. "Remember, it doesn't matter what it looks like, only how good it tastes."

She missed her mother so much.

Someone sat next to her and pulled her into a warm embrace. She rested her face against Jaewon's chest, breathing in his clean scent. The loneliness was chased away as she held on to him. There was a great comfort to be had in listening to the steady rhythm of his heartbeat and feeling his chest rise and fall with each breath. He was her solace in times of despair. She'd known him for only seven months and yet she couldn't imagine a time without him. How had he forced his way into her heart like this?

"When you were up in the Tiger's Nest Temple and I saw the mountain crumble down, I vowed that if you made it out alive, I would never leave your side again," Jaewon said.

"You're going to drive me crazy," she griped.

"Too bad! I nearly had a heart attack worrying over you. I'm not going through that again. I love you too much."

There were the words again. Kira straightened up, wiping away her tears.

"Will you run away from me every time I say I love you?"

"No, it's just that I'm not sure how to respond." Kira stared at her feet, afraid to look at him.

Jaewon cupped her face and kissed her, soft and gentle. He pulled away, leaving her aching for more, and stared into her eyes with a serious expression.

"I don't need you to say anything. I just need you to be with me. Can you do that for me? No matter how tiresome I might be?"

This time Kira reached up and kissed him.

Kira met with Brother Woojin privately to show him the last of the treasures.

"The Dragon King warned me that the belt is too powerful a weapon and should not be used at all. He told me the greatest danger is that the Demon Lord would use me and the belt to destroy the world."

The monk gazed with reverence at the treasure.

"These are the fourteen master dragons of the heavens. To wear this belt is to have the power to unleash them." He touched each of the jade dragons. "No wonder the Dragon King doesn't want it to be used. All fourteen dragons unleashed on the world at the same time would be too powerful, indeed! Look at them! The dragons of the sea, earth, air, fire. And the four dragons of the winds.

This one is the volcano dragon and here is the dragon of the frozen tundra. Lastly, these are the dragons of the north, south, east, and west."

Kira's eyes lingered on the dragon of the east, a silver dragon that reminded her of the Dragon King.

"This treasure is the most powerful piece in the world," the monk said. "And you must protect it carefully."

When he tried to place the belt into her hands, Kira pulled away and shook her head.

"I am weak. I cannot be responsible for such a dangerous weapon. I must ask you to hold on to it. Maybe we should send it to Dragon Springs Temple. I am now the worst person in the world to keep it safe!"

"My dear girl, I think you do yourself a grave disservice to think this way," Brother Woojin said. His face was troubled as he grasped her resisting hand and pressed the belt into it.

"Fate has brought the belt into your keeping. It is your duty and your responsibility now, no one else's." He pressed his hands over hers, holding them still. "Whatever is to happen now is up to you. To push this responsibility away may end up causing a worse outcome. But if you maintain control as the Dragon Musado, you will fulfill your destiny, whatever it may be."

"What if my destiny is to destroy the world?" she asked in despair.

"Then that is what is meant to happen," he replied. "But that does not mean the end of life. A new world will grow. Perhaps a better one. We do not know what is to happen."

Despite the monk's encouraging words, Kira was uneasy. She was not going to be the reason for the dragon apocalypse. But what could she do to protect herself from the Demon Lord?

She wandered the temple grounds and came upon a small hidden shrine for Gwaneum, the goddess of mercy. The golden statue depicted the beautiful, serene face of the goddess sitting next to a white tiger. All around the shrine's walls, there were multicolored murals of tigers. Here, Kira felt a great presence of peace. She gazed at Gwaneum's calm face and began to pray. She prayed for her parents' spirits and the hope that they would continue to watch over her and her brothers. She prayed for her aunt and uncle and asked them to protect Taejo. She prayed for her uncle Eojin to be released from the underworld and once again reunited with his family. As she prayed, a calm entered her soul. She knew that the prayers for all of her family members were being heard. Looking up at the statue, she suddenly felt the presence of her parents' spirits.

"Father? Mother?" Kira gasped. She closed her eyes and felt their presence with her.

"Little tiger, you will be fine," her mother whispered.

"My warrior girl! I am so proud of you, my child!" Her father's voice was so strong and deep.

She was so grateful to hear their voices again.

"I miss you so much," she said. "I need you. I don't know what to do. I don't want to fail."

"We are always with you," her mother said. *"You are not alone."*

"Kira." Her father spoke in his calm assured manner. *"Don't doubt yourself. You are my daughter and I believe in you. From the day you were born, you were always meant to do great things, to rise above even your own potential. You are our greatest hope. Remember the things I have taught you and you will not fail."*

The voices faded away and she knew that they had returned to heaven, but the warmth stayed with her.

"Thank you, Goddess of Mercy," she said as she prostrated herself in front of the statue. "If only I knew what to do about the jade belt."

After a long moment, she pushed herself up. As she did, she noticed a shift in the surface under her fingertips. The stone right under the white tiger's front paw was loose. She carefully lifted it up and found a hidden compartment inside. The space was small and completely tiled. Though it was empty, it had clearly been meant as a hiding place. A strong impulse overtook her.

She pulled the leather bag containing the belt out of her bust wrap and opened it. The jade belt gleamed in the late-afternoon sun. Kira looked at the silver dragon that was the dragon of the east. It was on the longest chain of the belt. Without pausing to think, Kira loosened the top link and pulled off the silver dragon on its chain. She looped it over her neck, hooked the open link onto the last link in the chain, and closed it, straining to get it as tight as possible. The silver dragon rested against her chest, sitting above the tidal stone. The belt now contained only thirteen dragons. She placed a hand on her chest and felt good about her decision. Wrapping the belt in its leather satchel, she placed it in the far corner of the compartment and then replaced the tile.

She heaved a sigh of relief. If she was captured, at least the belt would be safe. The world would be safe. No one would know that the dragon of the east rested against her chest. Why she took it, she didn't know. There was something comforting about the little figure. Maybe by having it with her, the wisdom of King Dang would impart itself to her.

She could only hope.

13

On the fifth day, a party of soldiers arrived from the Iron Army. It was Major Pak who summoned Kira from the guesthouse to come meet with the messenger. When she was brought to the temple, Kira was elated to see that the messenger was her brother Kwan.

"Oppa!" Kira shouted, her smile so big it actually hurt. It was so good to see him again.

His arms were wide open as she ran to him. He hugged her hard.

"Are you all right?" he asked.

"I'm perfectly fine!" Kira said. "But what about you? Are you completely healed from where Fulang clawed you?"

He patted his side gingerly. "It still hurts and I'm going to have an interesting scar, but I'm fine."

Just then, Taejo arrived with Brother Woojin, Jaewon, and Seung. The prince raced over to Kwan's side and gave him a big hug.

"It's good to see you again, my prince," Kwan said. "Especially because you are on the ground and not flying in the air, in the claws of a gigantic blue dragon!"

"I'm glad Noona rescued me," Taejo said, shooting Kira a grateful look. "I've never been so hungry in my life."

"Hungry? Not scared?" Kwan asked.

Taejo shook his head. "I knew Noona would come for me," he said simply. "I just had to be patient."

Kira reached over to tug at his hair, marveling at how tall he'd grown. "He's been eating nonstop since we got here. And he's gotten so tall. Sunim and I are busy trying to sew him some new clothes from the fabric that the monks left behind."

Kwan raised an eyebrow. "Will you be sewing him some monk's robes then and shaving his head?"

"No, don't be silly! Sunim found a whole chest full of silk cloth. He thinks it was a donation that the monks didn't have time to sell," Kira said.

"Oh, so you are going to deck him out in fancy robes and make us carry him around in a palanquin?"

Elbowing Kwan, she stopped his teasing with a hard look. "We are making him a black uniform," she said.

"It's like yours and Noona's!" Taejo piped in with a grin.

Kwan became serious and bowed his head. "A fitting uniform for you, my prince."

Suddenly, he straightened, his face turning hard.

"It's good to see you again," Jaewon said, as he approached them. "I'm glad to see you are healed from your wounds."

Kwan nodded abruptly, staring at Jaewon with a suspicious look. He studied first Jaewon and then Kira, as if he sensed some change between them.

"Tell me everything that happened on the island," he demanded. "Everything!" He stepped right up to Jaewon's face as he continued to eye him in an intimidating fashion.

Jaewon threw up his hands and stepped away. "I think I will let your sister answer that question," he said easily.

"No, that's a talk we can have in private later," Kira said. They engaged in a battle of wills, the two Kang siblings trying to outstare the other, until eventually Kwan backed down.

With a last nasty look at Jaewon, Kwan said, "I need to talk with Kira, our cousin, and Major Pak anyway."

Brother Woojin hurried over to hustle Jaewon out. "Then let us leave you to talk," he said, pushing Jaewon out the door, a grinning Seung following close after them. Kira caught Taejo's impish grin.

"It's going to be so fun now that your brother is here," Taejo whispered.

"Not for Kim Jaewon," she replied.

"That's why it's going to be fun," he said.

"Wait a minute—I thought you promised to help him," Kira said.

"And I will," he said. "But if he can't stand up to your brother, then he doesn't deserve you."

For a moment, Kira was speechless. He was no longer her little cousin. He'd grown into a worthy man.

"That's something my father would have said." Pride coursed through her as she studied him. "He would be so proud of you."

"We have heard that the daimyo is near Nosong, the Kudara capital, amassing a tremendous army against us," Kwan said. "Our spies tell us that Yamato fleets have been sailing around Tamna Island and landing at Mulhay at the very southeastern tip of the peninsula. We've always known that Kudara had joined forces with the Yamato, but now we must take the fight to them. We must once and for all drive them off our land. The Iron Army goes to war against Kudara! All the forces are heading for Nosong."

"Do we have enough men?" she asked.

Kwan nodded. "Much has happened. Our brother has been very busy. The Tongey prince, Prince Namhoe, has been given back his army, as well as some Iron Army troops. They make up the Fourth Division and Namhoe will command it. All other forces have rallied under our brother's command. Even General Kim."

Kira blinked to hear the general's name. He had tried to kill her when she was unable to save King Eojin. It was because of him that Kira had had to sneak out of Hansong. "Should I be worried about him?" she asked.

"He swore that if you saved the prince from the dragon and brought him home safely, then he would pledge his full support to our brother."

Kira was skeptical. General Kim was not someone she could ever trust. He'd gone slightly insane after King Eojin's death and she feared for his mental state.

Her brother noticed her expression. "I don't like it any better than you do, but we need every soldier for this coming battle. Even the rebel forces are coming together under our brother's command. They've been combined with General Kim's army and now form the Fifth Division. Our brother believes that what everyone now needs is to see the Musado and the prince at his side."

"I'm ready," Taejo said.

Kwan gave an approving nod. "We are going to march on Nosong. But all our forces will rendezvous in Muju. Kyoung is heading there with the First Division and a combined Hansong and saulabi army will make up the Second Division. The Third and Fourth Divisions will head into Asan from Hansong, about one hundred and forty li north of Nosong. Our spies say Asan is deserted. All the enemy forces retreated south."

"What about General Kim?" Kira asked.

"His men have been cleaning out the southern shores

of Jinhan and Kaya but are setting their course for Kudara as we speak. They will head straight to Nosong."

"How far is Muju from Nosong?" Major Pak asked.

"About one hundred sixty li, but over some mountainous terrain. With all our foot soldiers and cavalry, it will take us two to three days to get there. The Third and Fourth Divisions should be there sooner than us and will wait outside the city boundaries for our command."

"With two divisions heading to Muju, will we be able to supply everyone there?" Major Pak asked.

Kwan nodded. "It's still lightly populated and a large farming community. We should be fine."

As the major and Kwan began to talk logistics, Kira turned to Taejo. "Are you ready for all of this?" she asked.

Taejo nodded, his young face looking mature. "I don't want to hide behind your sword anymore, Noona. I want to fight for my throne. And I'll do whatever it takes to give my people hope."

Before she answered, Kwan turned to her. "As we prepare for battle, our top priority is figuring out how we will kill the daimyo."

"Are we sure that the daimyo is in Nosong?" Kira asked.

"Yes," he replied. "Our best spies have reported back to us. This is our chance to kill him once and for all. Our brother is leading the entire Iron Army to Nosong, and we will join him at Muju. We'll leave in the morning."

Kira suppressed a shiver. She needed to avoid the

daimyo at all costs. And yet, if she were to have any hope of freeing her uncle Eojin from the shadow world and winning this war, she would have to kill the daimyo.

But how would she do it without risking being controlled by him? Her visions flashed before her eyes again. All she saw was the death of everyone she loved. She would not let that happen.

Yet what could she do when the mere thought of the daimyo frightened her so much? How could she face him?

Kwan had brought a small unit of ten soldiers to escort them to Muju. The party rode out the next day, cutting through the mountainous terrain and heading north. Late afternoon, a scout returned, warning of another armed force on their route.

"Looks like rebel forces. They wear a headband around their foreheads with a black-and-gold dragon insignia," the scout said.

Surprised and hopeful at hearing the news, Kira pushed forward. "Dragon headband?" she asked. "I know them. That's the sign of the Dragon Fighters from up north. Take us to them immediately."

They approached the campsite, where they were stopped by armed patrols. Upon recognizing Kira, they allowed the group to pass. The campsite was quite large. The Dragon Fighters had doubled in size since last she had seen them. Men and women in various colored uniforms, all wearing the dragon insignia headbands. They rose to their feet in wary respect. Kira's party dismounted and approached a large soldier, barking orders at the others.

"Are you the leader of the Dragon Fighters?" Kira asked.

The soldier pivoted and shouted, "Commander! You have visitors!"

Kira surveyed the area. Beyond the bustling campsite, Kira spotted a small *ger*, one of the northern tents Shin Bo Hyun had raved about not so long ago. Then someone came out of the ger, standing in the sunlight. At first Kira couldn't see who it was. When she did, she paled, unable to believe her eyes. Shin Bo Hyun stood in front of her, with the same half smile as always, but looking completely different. His long silky hair was gone, cropped close to his head. It made him look more masculine and intimidating. His eyes gleamed when he spotted her. He walked over, his smile getting wider with every step.

"Are you for real or are you a ghost haunting me?" Kira asked. She reached over and poked his cheek. It had been over a month since she'd last seen him at the Yalu River.

Shin Bo Hyun held her hand against his chest. "See?

It's really me," he said, his eyes gazing intensely into hers.

Kira snatched her hand away, shaking her head in disbelief. "This is the second time I thought you were dead. But for the first time, I'm glad you aren't."

"That's definitely an improvement." He laughed. He looked back and waved Chansu over. "Apparently this one had been secretly tracking us. He rounded up the men we had sent off as decoys, and came after us. I don't think I would have made it if it wasn't for him."

Chansu bowed, but his eyes beamed fury and retribution. She remembered him well. His hatred of her was palpable as always.

Ignoring him, Kira turned to Shin. "But why are you here?" she asked.

"I pushed my men as hard as I could to head south to join your brother's army, as you requested. But instead, I cross paths with you again," he said. "It's fate. How can you doubt that we are destined to be together?"

"And what happened to your hair?" she asked, marveling at the changes in him.

He smiled ruefully, running a hand over his short hair. "I was very sick after the dunking in the Yalu and had a high fever. In order to cool off, I demanded that they shave my head. Being good soldiers, they listened to me, even in my delirious state." He sighed. "I look like a monk! But I have to admit, it is very comfortable."

Kira assessed him for a long moment. "It suits you. You look less noble and more like a soldier."

Shin's eyes gleamed in delight. "And what happened to your hair? I find it interesting that when we see each other again, we have both lost our long hair. Is this a coincidence or are we soul mates?"

Kira tugged at her short wavy hair. "My story is not as funny. I had to cut it to get a ride with the River God's daughters." She shrugged. "It's only hair. It'll grow back."

"You look cute and sweet and harmless," Shin said. "Very deceptive. I approve."

Kira choked. "Please, don't make me laugh."

Leaning close to her, Shin said, "It is good to see you again, Kang Kira. I have missed you."

She shook her head in disbelief. "I can't believe you're here. I thought you were dead."

"I'm pretty hard to kill," Shin bragged, winking at her.

"And after all you've been through, you still came all the way down here," she marveled.

"I told you, I would do anything for you and I meant it," Shin said with a serious gaze. "Please don't ever forget it."

As always, Kira found her reaction to Shin Bo Hyun puzzling and uncomfortable. She was grateful when her brother Kwan came charging up, his expression one of complete distrust.

"Shin Bo Hyun," he said in a reserved voice. "To what do we owe this honor?"

The other man inclined his head respectfully. "As I was explaining to your sister, my army is committed to join forces with the Iron Army against our mutual enemy. We were headed down to Dongnae, which is where we last heard the Iron Army was stationed."

"Then we welcome you," Kwan said. "The Iron Army is heading west to Kudara. You may march with us to Muju."

He then stepped closer to Shin, so that only Shin and Kira could hear him. "But know this: leave my sister alone or you will wish you had drowned in the Yalu River."

Kwan motioned for Kira to follow him. She left with a rueful shrug of her shoulders. Shin looked resigned to Kwan's distrust. As she walked through the campsite, she caught sight of a pair of amber eyes watching her.

"Nara! What are you doing here?" Kira exclaimed. She greeted the kumiho with an enthusiastic hug.

"I was curious about this man that you felt such guilt over," Nara said. "Once I knew you were in safe hands, I went looking for him and quite conveniently guided him to you."

Kira looked at the besotted faces of the men as they stared at the kumiho. She then gazed appraisingly at Nara, who was dressed in a red soldier's uniform and wearing the same dragon headband over her forehead. Even in uniform she looked gorgeous.

"Don't worry, I'm not up to my old tricks again." Nara smiled. "But I can't help it if they find me irresistible. I think I'll join you instead, although your brother may not approve."

"You will be one of many, then," Kira replied with a smirk.

As they walked outside Shin's campsite, Nara's uniform shimmered away and was replaced by a silvery blue hanbok, with her hair once again flowing down her back.

"Now that's much better," Nara said.

"Not very useful in a fight, though," Kira said.

Nara shot her a thoughtful look. "Not everything must be utilitarian," she said. "Beauty is an important part of life also, little sister. It makes life worth living. Don't you ever want to wear a fine silk hanbok and put your hair up with jeweled combs?"

Kira shook her head. "It is truly not important to me," she said. "But I do appreciate beauty. In fact, I like looking at you all dressed up like that. But it's not for me."

"How intriguing," Nara said. "It is refreshing to meet someone with so little vanity."

"Oh, I have vanity," Kira said. "Just not about my looks."

At their approach, Kwan, who was busy setting up camp, did a double take.

"Not you too!" he fumed. "This is turning into some mad circus."

"Does that mean you don't want my help?" Nara asked.

Kwan ignored her.

"Well then, I'll sit here and watch you work," she said, gracefully sitting on a fallen log.

Jindo, who had begun to growl at the kumiho, was hushed by Taejo. Brother Woojin kept Taejo close to his side, perplexed by Nara's appearance, while Seung avoided looking at her, preparing the evening meal with his back turned entirely to their new guest.

Seung called Kira over frantically. "What do I serve her for dinner?" he asked anxiously. "If she doesn't like what we have to eat, will she get hungry for something else?" His eyes had gotten round and panicky.

Kira swallowed a snort of laughter. "Don't worry, Seung. I promise she won't attack any of the men in our group."

After reassuring him, she saw that Gom wasn't frightened of Nara. He went over to sit by the kumiho, evidently fascinated by her. She smiled down at the dokkaebi and scratched his head, sending him into blissful raptures.

Kira noticed Jaewon slipping away. Seeing that Nara was now conversing with Taejo and Brother Woojin, she followed him.

She found him not too far away, sitting on a fallen log. He was carving a piece of wood again. It was a small statue of what looked like an animal.

"Why'd you run away?" she asked.

He refused to meet her eye.

"I needed a moment to myself," he said.

"You didn't even stick around to see Shin Bo Hyun and his army."

"There was no need for me to be there."

"You could have at least greeted him."

"I don't believe he cares if I greet him or not."

"You're probably right," she said. "Well, then, I'll leave you alone."

"You seem overly happy to see your betrothed again," he griped at her.

Kira's temper flared up. "First of all, he's not my betrothed! And secondly, I thought he'd died trying to save us. Of course I'm happy to see him! What kind of ridiculous comment is that?"

She turned to leave, but Jaewon put up a hand to stop her. "Tell me I have nothing to worry about, and I will believe you."

"I don't even know what you are worried about in the first place! Stop being ridiculous!"

With that, she stormed away, returning to the campsite in a fury.

"What's put you in such a foul mood?" Nara asked.

Kira didn't answer, walking out of earshot of the others. Nara followed her, watching as Kira paced back and forth.

"Someone's in a lot of trouble," Nara remarked.

"Kim Jaewon is an ass," Kira fumed. "I don't understand him. How was I supposed to react when seeing Shin Bo Hyun?"

The kumiho smiled. "You really have no idea about men," she said.

Kira arched an eyebrow. "I've spent my entire life surrounded by men. What's there to know?"

"You really need a female friend," Nara observed.

"I have you," Kira said.

Nara sighed. "I'm not quite the same, but I guess I'll have to do."

She reclined lazily against a large boulder. "Human emotions are so fascinating. Don't you see? He's insanely jealous."

"Jealous of what?"

"Because you are attracted to Shin Bo Hyun," Nara said.

Kira turned on the kumiho. "What? Are you crazy? I am most definitely not attracted to him!"

The kumiho gave her a wicked glance. "I've seen your thoughts, Kang Kira."

"*Aish!* Get out of my head, Nara!"

"We are connected. I can sense all your strongest thoughts, my friend."

"Then something is wrong with your senses because I don't like Shin Bo Hyun!"

"You don't have to like someone to find them attractive," Nara said.

"Don't be ridiculous! I would never have anything to do with him!"

"Why not? He is such a fine figure of a man," Nara purred. "I find him irresistible."

Kira gave her a dark look. "You sound like all the court

ladies that used to fawn over him. That's his problem. He knows too well how irresistible he is."

"Is that your problem? To be honest, I find a self-confident man so much more attractive than a man who is awkward and jealous like Kim Jaewon."

"There's nothing wrong with Jaewon!" Kira lashed out. "He is a great man, a far better one than Shin Bo Hyun could ever hope to be! I would take him over Shin any day!"

"Then you should tell him that yourself," Nara replied, "because that is what he wishes to hear."

Kira opened her mouth to object and then closed it quickly. Heaving a big sigh, she sat down next to Nara.

"The thing is, I really do care about Jaewon so much. I can't imagine life without him," Kira confided. "But he is a distraction that I don't need right now. I don't want to be thinking about him when I have so much I need to focus on. I have so much pressure on me that it makes me nauseous to think about it. And then he'll come along and make me laugh and forget about everything except these feelings he stirs up inside me. I get all confused and I lose focus."

"So you do love him," Nara said, her eyes gleaming in triumph.

"I don't know, I guess so," Kira said. "But I'm not ready to tell him. I'm supposed to be the Dragon Musado. I'm supposed to stop the daimyo and the Demon Lord, and there's a strong chance I won't survive the coming war.

He's been through so much pain, and I don't want to hurt him."

"Kira, my dear girl, there's no way around that," Nara said with a pitying look. "Anything you do is going to hurt him."

"Yes, but it would be worse for him to think we have a future and then have that taken away," Kira said. "That would be far worse."

The kumiho looked at her with a strange expression. "I'm not sure about that," she said. "I think the greatest tragedy is to never know you were truly loved. I am immortal, and I would give up my immortality to know what it is like to be in love. Even knowing how fleeting a human's life is."

Her words made Kira pause. How would she feel not knowing Jaewon's feelings for her? Her chest ached at the thought. But then she considered the unending pain she'd felt at the loss of her parents. She shook her head. "No, I can't hurt him like that. I'll tell him after all of this is done. If I'm still alive."

The kumiho turned her elegant shoulder and closed her eyes. "I hope you don't regret it."

15

The next day the Dragon Fighters joined in the march to Muju. Shin came up to ride next to Kira, to the great dissatisfaction of both Kwan and Jaewon. Major Pak was polite but distant, and Seung kept away out of loyalty to Jaewon. Even Taejo, who agreed that Shin had saved them at the Yalu River, avoided the young lord. Only Kira, Brother Woojin, and Nara would talk with him.

Unsurprisingly, none of this seemed to bother Shin Bo Hyun.

"I don't blame the prince for not speaking to me," he said. "He has lost everything because of my uncle."

"That would be true for all of us," she said in an even tone.

Shin gazed at her as he answered. "But you still have your brothers. The prince lost his family and his throne."

"Yes, you are right: he should hate you forever," she said.

Shin shot her a reproachful look. "You needn't be so cruel about it. It's not easy knowing your future king might want to exile or kill you."

Kira relented. "But that's not true. He is grateful for your help, Shin Bo Hyun," she said. "He just needs time to heal."

"And what of you?" he asked. "How much time do you need to heal?"

"What do you mean?"

He reached over from his horse and touched her face, tracing the scar along her eyebrow and down her cheek. Kira felt a fluttering sensation in her chest that she crushed down ruthlessly. She had no intention of having her feelings confused by Shin Bo Hyun again.

"Will you ever forgive me?" he asked.

Kira looked at him. "My lord, I forgave you when you sacrificed yourself at the Yalu River to save the prince."

Shin turned his head. He opened his mouth to speak, but an alarmed shout from the front guard interrupted him.

"Ambush!" a soldier cried, as a split second later an arrow shot into his throat. Right before their eyes, the soldier turned black and hard, and became frozen as a statue, falling off his horse. It was a cursed arrow, just like the ones that had killed King Eojin.

Some of Shin's soldiers raced forward from the back.

"Demon soldiers have ambushed us, sir!" a woman soldier said. "They've cut us off from the rest of the Dragon Fighters!"

"They're trying to surround us," Kira said. "We must protect the prince!"

She raced over to Taejo's side, pulling out her bow and arrow. The soldiers surrounded the prince, while Dragon Fighters took the outer circles. Taejo pulled out his sword, his face determined.

"I'm ready for them," he said.

Kira sternly shook her head. "I know you are, but they are shooting cursed arrows. There is no defense from them."

Then another arrow took out a man to Taejo's right. They watched in horror as he turned into a statue, causing his horse to bolt. The other soldiers closed their circle tighter, but it wasn't enough. Kira couldn't watch as the enemy picked off all their men. She had to do something.

Major Pak, Jaewon, Seung, and Brother Woojin were now surrounding the prince along with several of Shin's Dragon Fighters. Kira could see the panic in Taejo's eyes. He was trying to be brave, but it had to be terrifying. This was how their uncle, King Eojin, had died. Taejo had seen exactly how agonizing their uncle's last moments were. She would not let anything happen to Taejo.

"You must protect the prince," she yelled.

Jaewon made a move to come with her, but Kira stopped him. "No, I beg you! You need to guard the prince no matter what happens to me. Please!"

For a moment, an expression of pure torture passed over his face. He nodded grimly.

Kira leaped off her horse and raced toward the lines of battling soldiers. Looking down, she saw Gom running by her side.

"No, Gom, you must stay with the prince and protect him!" Kira told the dokkaebi. "Don't leave him until I order you to do so!"

Kira tried to pinpoint where the arrows were coming from and charge toward it. Several half-breeds tried to intercept her, but she cut them down with brutal efficiency. Her entire focus was on stopping the archer, now hidden by the thick foliage of the trees and brush.

Shin Bo Hyun leaped off his horse and raced to her side.

"What are you doing? Are you crazy?" he shouted.

"We have to stop that archer!" Kira yelled.

They fought side by side, Kira's eyes sweeping the woods as she fought off her attackers. As they thundered closer, Kira barely missed deflecting a blow to her head.

"Watch out, Kira!" Shin shoved her head out of the way as he skewered a half-breed through the neck. Several of Shin's soldiers finally broke through the wall of enemies and raced to their aid.

Right at that moment, Kira saw it. A rustle of leaves

rained down as an arrow came shooting out of the branches of a cherry tree ahead. Dropping her sword, she whipped out her bow and released two arrows in rapid succession. A body fell out of the trees, but not before he had released an arrow heading straight toward Shin.

"Watch out!" Kira shoved Shin out of its path and felt the excruciating pain of the cursed tip as it ripped through her forearm.

"Kira!" Shin shouted, then speared the half-breed that came up behind her, killing him instantly.

Even as more half-breeds converged on them, Kira couldn't focus on anything but the searing pain in her blackening arm. She gripped her arm tightly below her elbow and begged the tidal stone for help. *Get rid of the curse!*

The tidal stone burned hot against her chest. Kira wrenched the arrow from her arm. A scream of anguish slipped from her lips as she lost momentary connection with the stone. She was one massive ball of pain. She threw off her coat and tore off her sleeve, desperate to see what was happening. The black was spreading up her arm and down into her hand, and the ringing in her head was getting louder. She fell to the ground, trying desperately to fight off the curse, to stop it from spreading. If it reached her head, she knew it would be all over. Using the power of the tidal stone to fight the evil that was now in her blood, Kira was in a desperate battle for her life.

The half-breeds moved closer, trying to reach her.

Shin and the Dragon Fighters beat them back, but more and more surrounded them, cutting the Dragon Fighters off from Kira. Even as Shin fought madly to get back to her, she felt one of the half-breeds dragging her away by her feet.

Suddenly, Nara appeared in her fox form, snarling at the half-breed, her nine vivid tails bristling. She attacked him viciously, driving the creature away. But even as Nara chased down one, another came and pulled Kira by her leg.

"Kira!" Shin shouted. "You must fight! Don't let them take you!"

She didn't have the strength to fight. Her focus was solely on trying to stop the curse, but she was losing. The black had completely enveloped her arm from shoulder to fingertips and was now creeping up her neck. Soon it would spread into her head and she would die.

She heard Nara yelping in pain and the frantic calls of Shin and her brother. She turned her head in panic and spotted Kwan trying to get to her, fighting through the enemy soldiers. Jaewon's voice called out her name over and over.

And then she stopped moving.

There was a thunderous roar. A new army joined the battle, as a dokkaebi smashed in the head of the half-breed that had captured her. Moments later, her personal army was attacking the half-breeds with gusto. Grateful to see them, Kira hoped it wasn't too late. She begged the tidal stone to help her.

Jaewon was the first to reach her side. He gasped as he took in the smooth black marble that was her arm. He reached over to touch it, but Kira pushed him away.

"Don't touch me!" she cried. Her brother's finger was forever stone from touching the cursed blade. She couldn't let that happen to Jaewon.

"Water, I need water," she pleaded.

He ran to get a water bag, and by the time he returned, Shin was holding her up in his arms.

"On my wound," Kira begged. "Quickly!"

Shin took the bag from Jaewon's hands and poured it over her arm. Kira screamed as the water that touched the black wound began to bubble. Huge blisters formed over her skin. The tidal stone was singing in her head, trying to quiet the curse. It vibrated against her skin.

"More water," Kira gasped.

This time the water steamed at contact. The pain that had been creeping up her neck began to recede. The blackened, blistered skin began to peel off, leaving new pale skin behind. Red blood poured out of the wound. Knowing she'd done all she could do to rid her body of the curse, Kira felt her consciousness fade.

"Bind her arm, she's losing too much blood," Shin said.

"Kira, can you hear me?" Jaewon's voice was shaky.

"Let's get her out of here," Shin said.

She felt herself being carried and saw Shin's hard jaw at eye level. Over his shoulder, she took in Jaewon's anguished face. Behind him, Nara's fox form lay on the ground, her amber eyes blinking in pain.

"Nara," Kira whispered. She couldn't leave her friend behind. She tried to twist out of Shin's arms when she began to convulse in agony. The curse had seeped into her brain, spreading the blackness inside her. She could hear the Demon Lord's evil laughter reverberating even as the screaming grew louder.

And then she remembered no more.

16

She was back in the tunnel in front of the iron door, watching as it was smashed apart. This time, she didn't even have the chance to try and stop it. The fury of the creatures sent the iron door flying open as dark things poured screaming out. Black, furry creatures with yellow fangs and red eyes engulfed her, shrieking and moaning, desperate for a taste of her. They covered every inch of her skin, biting her, ripping off chunks of her flesh. There was no time to scream. She was being eaten alive.

She woke in a feverish state. Her body was burning. She tore at her clothes, desperate to escape the heat. Hands held her firmly, giving her water to drink. She was in a moving cart, and the swaying motion made her sleepy. Closing her eyes, she slipped away again.

The monstrous form was smothering her, sucking the air out of her lungs. She couldn't see it but it surrounded her. It felt like a hundred bodies pressed upon her. Kira's rib cage fractured and her lungs were collapsing. Despair such as she'd never known crushed her soul. And as she was dying, she saw the land all around her was a barren—a wasteland of death and destruction.

She dreamed all the time. Nightmares and visions. Unlike the last time she had encountered the cursed blades with her uncle Eojin, Kira didn't hear the voice of the Demon Lord. But her nightmares were far worse. She would wake up screaming every hour. At one point, she imagined her wound turning black again, spiders crawling out of her skin and into her mouth.

Cold sweat covered her as she tried desperately to rip off the dressing on her arm. Gentle hands stopped her. She saw Seung's round face looking down at her with concern and Jaewon holding her firmly in his arms. She collapsed against him, weeping until she passed out again.

The nightmares were horrendous, spiraling out of control and sending Kira into madness. In between her nightmares, she recalled seeing and hearing people by her side.

She was in a bright room that she didn't recognize. The thick papered walls and sliding door indicated that she was in a house of a well-to-do family. She felt the warmth emanating from the heated floor. And yet she still shivered uncontrollably.

Kwan and Taejo were there, Gom sniffling at his side.

"Why isn't he staying with her? I thought he was supposed to stay by her side."

"She told him that he had to stay with me until she ordered him otherwise. You can see how badly he wants to stay with her," Taejo said. "But don't worry, I spend most of my time here."

"You need sleep too, and no one can get any rest around her," Kwan said grimly.

"Sunim and I can hear her even from the other wing of the house," Taejo said. "She screams all day and night."

"Her dreams must be terrifying," Kwan said. "I've never seen her so badly affected."

"I don't understand, why isn't she healing already?"

"It was a cursed arrow."

Kira suddenly knew why her tiger spirit wasn't visiting her. If they were constantly with her, then the spirit would not come. But she couldn't speak, she couldn't tell them. All she could do was sleep.

The next time she opened her eyes, she was gasping for breath. Something heavy was on her chest. There was an intense aroma of ginger and mint. She tried to push it off, but it wouldn't budge. Panicking, she forced herself up.

Seung's face swam into view.

"You must lie down, young mistress. We have to keep the hot compress on you. It will help you."

She shook her head, trying to tell Seung that she couldn't breathe. Jaewon was there, gently forcing her down.

"It's OK, we're right here," Jaewon said. "You have to get some rest."

He held her hand as Seung reapplied the heavy heated compress to her upper chest. Kira gripped Jaewon tightly and closed her eyes.

She woke up screaming. Faceless monsters covered her flesh and feasted on her eyes. They crawled into her ears, nose, and mouth. Kira clawed at her face, trying to free herself of them. They wriggled their way into her cavities and down her throat.

This time a woman servant she'd never seen before tried to hold her hands down, making soothing noises at her. Another servant held a bowl of cold water, trying to wipe Kira's face. It smelled of ginger and ginseng.

Kira knocked over the bowl, shrieking that the monsters had consumed her. She shoved the woman off her and continued to claw at her face. Blood began to ooze down her neck. One of the women hurried out the door and returned with her brother. He held her down as she raged at him, pleading for him to kill the monsters. There were tears in his eyes and she wondered why he was crying.

Finally, she returned to sleep.

She'd lost all concept of time. When she next woke,

she saw her brother Kwan sitting by her side.

"Water," she whispered.

Kwan scooped out some water from a nearby bucket and held the ladle up to Kira's lips.

"How are you feeling?" he asked.

"Terrible," she croaked. "Where are we?"

"We are in Muju. We beat our brother here. I was grateful to find this estate. The family had left, but the servants were still here."

"How long have I been sick?"

"For nearly three days," Kwan said. "I don't understand—why aren't you healing as usual?"

"You have to leave me alone for an entire night," she said. "My tiger spirit won't come unless I'm alone."

"I didn't realize," he said. "You've been having such horrible nightmares, so I thought it was important to have someone with you."

Kira shook her head. "Please, leave me for a while."

He leaned over to check her wound first. Pulling open the dressing, he exposed angry red lines that shot out from the puncture wound, a clear sign of poison. But there were no signs of black. He then looked her face over carefully.

"You scratched your face up real good," he said. Caressing her hair, he rose to his feet. "I was so frightened." He stopped and cleared his throat. "Get better soon."

Kira stopped him. "Wait. Where's Nara? Is she OK?"

"I don't know. When we went back to find her body, it was gone. I'm sure she's all right."

Kira was troubled, hoping the kumiho had made it to safety.

After he had left, Kira closed her eyes and begged her tiger spirit to come. It was not long afterward that she felt its soothing presence. Opening her eyes, she was relieved to see the golden halo of light that surrounded her now. Already, the pain was starting to slip away.

Someone was shaking her awake.

"Wake up! Hurry! You must wake up!"

Kira opened her eyes to see Chansu's nervous face.

"What are you doing here?" she asked, still groggy from sleep.

"You must come quickly!" He yanked urgently at Kira's arm. "The prince has wandered into the forest and is in terrible danger."

Kira got up, still shaky and not completely healed. It was dark outside and she had been with her tiger spirit for only a few hours. But she still felt better than before.

"What happened? Where's my brother?" she asked.

"He and his men are in the forest," Chansu replied. "He sent me to get you immediately. You must come now!"

Without waiting for her response, Chansu ran out her door and down the hallway.

"Chansu, wait!"

Kira stumbled from the house, strapping her sword and bow and arrows onto her back. Chansu was at the courtyard gate, waving at her to hurry.

"Young mistress, you mustn't leave," an older servant woman said in alarm. "You are still very sick."

Kira recognized the woman who had been taking care of her. "I must go. The prince is in trouble," she said.

The cold night air helped to wake her as she raced after Chansu, following the light of his lantern. They were now deep in the forests of Muju.

"Chansu, what happened? How is the prince in danger?" Kira asked.

"You'll see soon enough!" he yelled over his shoulder.

The terrible feeling of danger was churning in her stomach as Kira tried not to panic. She desperately wanted to know what had happened, but Chansu would not answer her questions. Fear gripped her as she wondered if something truly horrible had happened. Something the soldier was unable to even speak of.

When she thought she could no longer take not knowing, Chansu entered a clearing and came to an abrupt stop. The acrid stench of demon magic filled her nose. She seized her sword and circled the empty clearing.

"Chansu, be careful," she said. "There's a demon nearby."

She saw him take an unsteady step and glance around, a look of apprehension on his face.

Suddenly the air in the middle of the clearing began to shimmer. Kira's gut wrenched violently at the immediacy of the danger. A dark robed figure began to materialize.

"Chansu, come here now!" Kira shouted. "Dokkae—"

Kira was gripped in a magical paralysis. She tried to scream, but even her voice was frozen and her breath came in harsh rasps. Her sword fell from nerveless fingers and she fought desperately for control that was no longer hers.

She looked to Chansu for help, but was aghast to find the young soldier smiling.

"Well done, my son," the figure said as he raised his head to reveal the face of the daimyo. "You've brought me the Demon Slayer."

"And you promise to keep my master safe?" Chansu asked. "Lord Shin Bo Hyun won't be hurt?"

"Of course," the daimyo said. "Your master will become a great and powerful king. And you will be his first in command."

Kira stood in shock, staring at the gleeful face of the young man who now circled her.

"You think I'm a traitor, don't you? But I'm not. I'm protecting my lord from you!" Chansu spat, his face twisting with hatred. "You left him to die twice now, but never again. I would betray you a thousand times so that you would die and leave my lord alone!"

"And very wise of you, my young man," the daimyo said. "You have made the right decision." A look of pure evil crossed the daimyo's scarred face. "Come here, my dear."

The daimyo gave a careless flick of his finger and Kira found her body flying toward him through the air, unable to stop.

"Finally, the Demon Slayer, or should I say Dragon Musado?" He chuckled. "But what does it matter what I call you? You are mine now."

The daimyo was now solidified and he reached for her. The little bag containing the tidal stone and her *hae-tae* figurine were ripped off her neck and went flying into his hand. In the next moment, the jeweled dagger flew out of its scabbard and rested in the daimyo's grasp.

"Where is the dragon belt? Why is it not on you?"

Kira couldn't respond.

"No matter, we will find it. Now you will come to us and control the Dragon King's treasures for my lord and master," he said.

The loss of the treasures was crushing. She tried desperately to fight, but just like in her dreams, she was completely paralyzed.

Inside, she screamed for her tiger spirit.

The air about her shimmered and from above her head, her tiger spirit leaped out to attack the daimyo. It was the second time she'd seen her tiger spirit manifest into a physical form. It was larger than any real tiger and stood between Kira and the daimyo. Even as she watched the tiger and the shaman battle, Kira was frozen in place, her paralysis absolute. The daimyo was too powerful. She'd been so foolish to think she had a chance against him.

With a tremendous roar, the tiger clawed at the daimyo's chest, ripping away an amulet and smashing it under its paw. The daimyo's form immediately began to shimmer away. But before he disappeared completely, he formed a lightning ball between his hands and directed it at the tiger.

The air smelled of burning as Kira was released from the daimyo's control. She fell down next to the tiger's electrocuted body. At first, all she could do was stare in disbelief. This was her tiger spirit. How could it be dead? It felt as if a piece of her soul had been ripped out of her body. Her sobs were too painful to hold in. Steam rose from the body as Kira cradled the great cat's head. Only then did she begin to scream in rage and agony.

Her dokkaebi army appeared first, milling around in confusion, no enemy to be found. Moments later the clearing filled with soldiers as her brother, Jaewon, and Shin Bo Hyun came to her aid. Gom was leading the way.

Kwan and Jaewon knelt by her side. "What is it, what happened?" Kwan asked.

She raised her head, still heaving from her sobs. "This is my tiger spirit." She spoke brokenly.

There was a gasp of shock from all who saw her. They were staring at her eyes.

"Your eyes! What happened to them?" Jaewon gasped. "They're brown!"

Her heart seemed to freeze at his words. Her yellow eyes, her cursed yellow eyes were always her connection to her tiger spirit. If they were gone, then this truly meant her tiger spirit was dead.

Suddenly, the tiger's body began to shimmer, a golden light surrounding it. Ever so slowly, the tiger began to fade until there was nothing left. Kira's body began to shake. Something within her snapped. The grief was too painful and it overcame her—swiftly changing to rage and hate.

Kira turned wildly until she saw Chansu cringing against the base of a towering tree. Racing over to him, she punched him in the face, and began to beat him furiously into the ground.

"What are you doing?" Shin Bo Hyun shouted. He pulled Kira off the young soldier, who had not tried to defend himself.

"He did this to me! He betrayed me! He led me into a trap with the daimyo, who stole the treasures and tried to control me! He would have had me too but for my tiger spirit."

Kira began to weep uncontrollably. "My tiger spirit is dead because of him! He might as well have killed me!"

Shin Bo Hyun pushed Chansu away in shock.

"Why?" he asked. "Why would you betray us like this?"

"I would never betray you!" Chansu cried. "Only her! She is evil and must be destroyed!"

Shin stepped away, shaking his head. "You're not in your right mind. You don't know what you are saying," he said. "Tell me you were possessed when you did this! Tell me!"

"I did it for you!" he cried. "Everything I did was for you! She nearly killed you twice, and she'll do it again. She doesn't care about you. She only cares about the prince! I had to protect my lord. And you'll see! The daimyo will protect you! He'll make you king. You deserve to be king! More so than that pathetic little boy."

"You speak treason," Shin whispered.

"No, I speak the truth!"

"How could you do this?" Shin spoke in a daze. "You were like a brother to me!"

"I did it all for you, my lord!"

Kira saw the agony and rage on Shin Bo Hyun's face as he drew his sword.

"No!" Kira shouted. Launching to her feet, she placed herself between them, stopping Shin from striking the killing blow.

"He deserves to die! He is a traitor!"

"Then it should be at my hand," she said fiercely.

Shin's eyes refocused on hers, remorseful and guilty. He pressed a hand to her cheek and nodded.

Kira faced the traitor who knelt on the ground, his head hanging low. She grabbed hold of her sword and held it to his neck. Chansu raised his face and glared at her from eyes filled with both fear and hate.

"I'm not sorry for what I did," he spat at her. "My only regret is that you aren't dead!"

Kira had to fight back tears; she would not let him see her cry anymore. The urge to kill him was powerful and overwhelming, and she fought it internally. Fighting against her anger and the dark place from where it came. His death would not bring back her tiger spirit. It would be murder for revenge. That was not her way. It was not how her father had trained her. There was already so much death. Kira was tired of killing.

She put down her sword and took a step away.

"Go now, and never return." She spoke in a dull voice, all emotion and energy stripped of her.

Chansu's expression was one of utter disbelief.

"You're not going to kill me?"

"If I ever see you again, I will not hesitate to kill you. But right now, all I want is for you to be gone."

He rose to his feet hesitantly. Backing away, he threw a pleading look at Shin.

"My lord . . ."

"Didn't you hear what she said?" Shin roared. "Get out of here and never show your face again. Go before I kill you myself!"

Chansu fled.

In the quiet that ensued, no one moved. They were all waiting for Kira to react. All she could do was stare down at the spot where her tiger spirit had been.

Her brother tried to comfort her. "Kira, let's leave this place. Come, let's go back to the house," he said.

Without a word, she left the clearing, returning to her room.

It was Kwan who sat with her as she slept, while Gom

stayed curled up at her feet. When she woke, they were still there. Unwilling to talk to them, she sent them both away.

Not long after, Taejo and Brother Woojin came but Kira refused to talk to them.

Even when Jaewon knocked at her door, she didn't speak. She didn't move. She lay on her pallet and covered her head with her blanket, too tired to cry anymore. She had never felt so vulnerable in her life. The death of her tiger spirit was as devastating as the loss of her parents. It was as if part of her soul had been ripped out and destroyed. She fell into a trancelike depression. No matter who spoke to her, she didn't have the energy to respond.

"I need to go find our brother," Kwan said. "But I don't want to leave you like this."

Kira closed her eyes, hoping he would go away.

"Kira, you're scaring me," he said. "Please talk to me!"

But Kira had no words anymore. She was empty.

He sighed and stepped outside. She heard him talking with the others.

"Major Pak, I know your first duty is to the prince, especially with my sister like this, but you must keep an eye on her until I return," he said. "The dokkaebi army and Gom will keep all of you safe, but please check in on her. I must find my brother. She needs him. I will be as quick as I can."

Kira stayed in her room. She barely ate. Only Gom

and the women servants came in and out of her room.

Taejo slipped into her room and sat with her for an hour. He soon left when all his efforts were met with silence.

Out in the hallway, she heard him speaking tearfully to Brother Woojin. "She won't talk to me," he said.

Brother Woojin responded in a soothing voice. After a while, they left.

Relief. All she wanted was to be left alone. She drifted in and out of consciousness.

Someone knocked on her door.

"Kang Kira, I promised your brother I would check on you," Major Pak said through the closed door.

Her eyes were open, but her lips refused to speak.

"The servants say you're not eating," he said. "I'm growing quite concerned. You must eat something."

She still didn't answer. Eventually, he went away.

Sleep brought no comfort. She had disturbing dreams but none she could remember. All she was left with was the feeling of alarm and danger. She was so tired. She wondered if a person could sleep themselves into death.

The little dokkaebi was worried about her. He would scratch at her door incessantly until a female attendant would let him in. He would fetch Kira all sorts of treats like berries, nuts, pears, and cherries.

She ate nothing.

What she wanted nobody could ever give her.

"Gom," she said, her voice raspy. "Go watch over the

prince and don't leave his side until I tell you to."

Gom gave her a reproachful look but did as she commanded. The silence lasted another hour.

There was another knock on her door.

She ignored it. More knocking. The door slid open and someone entered.

Kira closed her eyes against the intrusion. She felt someone sit next to her.

"I'm so sorry for what was done to you. Can you ever forgive me?"

It was Shin Bo Hyun.

Rage swept through her. How dare he come into her room? How dare he try and talk to her? He had no right to be there. It was all his fault. If he hadn't come back, she would never have lost her tiger spirit. Kira threw off her covers and stood up. She had to get away from him before she did something she would regret. Before she could walk away, Shin rose onto his knees and embraced her waist, pressing his face against her stomach. Her rage spiraled out of control and she began to tear herself away, but then she felt the wetness of his tears. They seeped into her jacket. Shin Bo Hyun crying? She was shocked. Her anger dissipated, leaving her exhausted and numb.

Kira placed a tentative hand on his head, caressing his soft, short hair. His arms tightened around her, as his shoulders shook with grief.

When he was finally calm, he rose to his feet, wiping his eyes on his sleeves.

"Kang Kira, my emotions are overwhelmed. Once again because of me you have suffered a grievous harm. The right thing to do would be to stay as far away from you as possible. And yet, I find that an impossibility," he said, "for my feelings for you have not changed."

He rubbed his knuckles down her scarred cheek and looked deep within her eyes. "No, that's not true. They have changed. They've become stronger than I could have ever known. I have loved you since I was eight years old. Time will not change this. And all I've ever wanted is to be by your side for the rest of my life."

Kira stared in amazement.

He pulled her into his embrace again. "I want to take care of you. I want you to enjoy life, not constantly worry about battling the enemy. I want to take you away from all of this so you can stop worrying about the prince and start to think about yourself. Think of a future. Come with me. Be with me. Let your brothers worry about this war. Let me worry about you from now on."

His words seduced her. They were exactly what she wanted to hear at that very moment. To lose all of her burdens and disappear. Mesmerized by his words, she stared at his mouth. He lowered his face and kissed her with firm lips that demanded a response. It was a kiss completely different from the ones with Jaewon. It was strong and confident and electric. But wrong. So wrong. Kira pushed him away and crossed her arms over her chest, willing her heart to calm itself.

"I'd like to be alone now, please," she said, not looking at him.

After a pause, he dropped a kiss on the top of her head and headed for the door. As he slid the door open, he turned around again. A small wrapped parcel in a wooden bowl was in his hands, and he brought it to her.

"Someone must have left this for you," he said. After one last lingering look, he exited the room.

Kira took the parcel out of the bowl and unwrapped it. Inside, she found a tiny wood carving of a beautiful tiger bleached white with black stripes. She knew immediately it was from Jaewon. He must have come while she was with Shin. She wondered how much he'd overheard, and how hurt he must feel. Too emotionally exhausted by her own feelings, Kira lay down on her bed. Holding the little tiger tight in her hands, she fell into a deep, uneasy sleep.

17

The next day Kwan returned with Kyoung and a squadron of soldiers. The rest of the Iron Army would arrive in the following week, but Kyoung had come early with Kwan to comfort Kira.

Seeing Kyoung again reminded her of the pain of her loss. She spent the morning weeping in her oldest brother's arms.

Kyoung didn't say much, but having his comforting presence there was a balm to Kira's broken soul. Her brothers spent half the day sitting with her in her room, forcing her to eat.

"Kira, we will not leave until you eat," Kyoung said.

"You are wasting away and losing your muscle. This is unacceptable for a soldier. Don't make me force-feed you!"

She took the bowl of rice gruel with chicken and vegetables and forced herself to take a bite. When she tried to put the bowl down, her brother wouldn't let her.

Her temper flared. "I don't want to eat!"

There was a soft knock on the door. Kyoung opened it and Seung entered, carrying a small tray. He beamed happily to see her up. "It is so good to see you so much better, young mistress!" Seung said. He poured hot tea out into a small tea bowl and handed it to her. Kira shuddered and made a face as she smelled the potent mix of ginseng and honey.

"I know you are not a fan of ginseng," Seung said, "which is why I added a lot of honey. Please drink this. It will make you feel much better."

Kira felt her temper rising, but she looked at Seung's pleasant face and didn't want to hurt him. She took the tea bowl and quickly downed the ginseng mixture, scalding her tongue on the hot tea. She shuddered as it went down.

Giving Seung a sickly smile, she thanked him. Seung's joyful face made up for the awful taste.

"I will let Master Jaewon know that you drank all the tea," Seung said. "He will be so happy to hear it. He has been so worried for you."

With a deep bow, Seung quickly left the room.

"Good girl," Kyoung said. "Now eat this."

"Leave me alone!"

"We'll go away if you eat all of this." Kyoung pushed the full bowl in front of her face.

"I'm not hungry."

"You've starved yourself so badly that your body doesn't feel hunger. This is false. You need to eat and we will not leave until you finish the entire serving," Kyoung said.

Kira was furious, but seeing the determined expressions on their faces, knew she had no choice. "If I eat this, you'll leave me alone?" she asked.

"Until dinnertime," Kyoung agreed.

With an aggrieved huff, Kira quickly downed the bowl of gruel.

Satisfied, her brothers reluctantly departed.

Lying down gave Kira no satisfaction. Now that she'd eaten, she had a surge of energy that she'd not had in a while. She felt a sudden need to escape her room. Outside, the air was brisk and cool. Kira walked around her courtyard, taking deep cleansing breaths. She walked the entire length of the house, heading to the other wing, where Taejo and Brother Woojin were staying. Standing at their doorway, she could hear the monk teaching Taejo his lessons. Unwilling to bother them, she slipped away.

Still restless, she decided to step out of the walled gate and into the village streets of Muju. Here she saw the most visible proof of her brother Kyoung's arrival. Squadrons of Iron Army soldiers were stationed all over the streets.

At her appearance, the chatter on the streets died down. Most of the soldiers bowed, others stared in open-mouthed surprise.

"Her eyes aren't yellow!"

"She's just a normal girl now!"

"Then she can't be the Dragon Musado anymore. What use is she to us?"

The last comment hit her hard. This was what she had feared. Hearing it out in the open seemed to substantiate her own feelings. How could she face the daimyo or the Demon Lord? How was she to fight them? Without her tiger spirit, she was nothing special. Without the Dragon King's treasures, she could not win. What good was she to anyone anymore?

She'd made a mistake. Turning back, she quickly entered her courtyard gate and ran into the house.

18

That night, Kira's dreams were a mishmash of nightmares. Her sense of hopelessness was overwhelming. And through it all, she heard the voice of the Demon Lord mocking her once again. In the morning, bleary-eyed and exhausted from grief and sleeplessness, Kira woke to find Nara lounging beside her, cooling herself with a pretty wooden fan.

"Nara, you're safe! I was so worried about you!" Kira said, happy to see her friend.

"I had to go to my lair and give myself time to heal," Nara said. "I'm sorry I was not here when you needed me."

"It's not your fault," Kira said. "You were injured

protecting me. Thank you, my friend."

The kumiho caught Kira's hands between her own. "I will always be your friend. You are like a little sister to me. And I will always cherish you."

Kira blinked back the tears that threatened to fall again. "I am no longer special. I've lost my tiger spirit. I'm no longer the Dragon Musado."

"No, my little sister," Nara said. "You are still you. That has not changed. I can see inside you and this I know."

"You're wrong," Kira said. "Without my tiger spirit, I am nobody."

The kumiho slapped her fan shut and sat up straight, her amber eyes sparking with anger. "Are you disagreeing with your older sister?" Nara snapped. "How disrespectful! I've lived for many centuries now. Respect your elders, child."

"I'm sorry, Nara," Kira said. She was so tired. She didn't want to argue. There was no point. Nothing could change now.

Nara fanned herself again. "I have seen visions of the future again and they have stayed the same. Even with your loss, my visions have not changed! Why do you think that is?"

"I don't know," Kira said.

"Because you are still the Dragon Musado. If you were truly powerless, then I would have foreseen a new vision, a new future. It would have meant that you were somehow weakened. But I have seen no such visions. Therefore, nothing of significance has changed."

It was not that Kira didn't believe her friend. She wanted to believe her, but it was difficult to believe in the face of the impending doom that gripped her. The whispers of the Demon Lord that had filled her with her worthlessness throughout the long night.

Nara rose to her feet in a fluid motion. "You've been hiding in this room, shutting people out for too long. It is time for you to listen."

She returned a few minutes later with Brother Woojin.

"Sunim, I don't know what to do anymore," Kira said.

Brother Woojin sat staring at her, his kind eyes steadying her.

"I have faith, for you are still here, my child," he replied.

"I am no longer the Dragon Musado, as I don't have any of the treasures. I am useless."

He shook his head and reached out to clasp her hands between his. "You have always been too hard on yourself. Your tiger spirit is not dead, my child. It is still within you. But now it is helping you in a different way."

Kira shook her head. "I have failed. You cannot count on me anymore."

"Stop that at once!" This was the first time that Brother Woojin had ever yelled at her in anger. "You are the Musado! That cannot be taken away from you! Shaman Won was right to be disappointed in me. He was right to say that I was looking to the prince as our hero. And I am ashamed of it. But I can see clearly now. The prince is important, yes, but not as important as you. You will be legend. Even without your tiger spirit, can you not see that you are the source of power? The Demon Lord may have the Dragon King's treasures, but he cannot use them without you. He needs you to win this battle. As long as you stay out of his hands, we have a chance of winning!"

The quiet between them grew as Kira pondered his words. It was true that the daimyo could not use the treasures without her. He himself had indicated that. It was why they kept trying to take her alive. There was still something she might be able to do.

"He doesn't have all the treasures," Kira said quietly. "I hid the jade belt in a safe place."

The monk put his hands together as if in prayer. "Then we must make sure that he never gets his hands on you or the belt. And we will be saved."

"But it's not enough," she said, her expression grim. "He and the daimyo must be destroyed. That I know for certain."

"And who will destroy them if you believe you are not the Musado?" he asked.

She sat up straight and looked him directly in the eyes. "I may not be the Musado anymore, but, believe me, I will destroy them or die trying."

"Come with us," Kyoung said. "And bring your weapons."

Kira dragged herself to her feet and followed her brothers out of her house. They took her through the narrow city streets to what was the local magistrate's compound. Kyoung had taken it over as the command center for his men. He took them to a large walled-in courtyard and asked not to be disturbed.

A part of Kira had been hoping Jaewon would be there. She felt a strong sense of disappointment when he wasn't.

"What are we doing here?" she asked.

"You've been moping around in your room for too

long. We leave for Nosong in a matter of days. I can't afford to have my strongest fighter go soft," Kyoung said. "It's time to see if you are still our father's daughter."

His words infuriated her. She was not in the mood for practice, and now she was too angry to be effective.

They fought with wooden staffs, spears, and swords, and then practiced archery.

At first, her mind played tricks on her, telling her that she was no good. Her shooting was off and she was careless and easily distracted. The more she tried, the angrier she got, until she threw down her bow and arrow in frustration.

Kyoung stopped her. "Giving up so soon?"

"I can't do this right now!" Kira's anger took her to the verge of tears. "I'm not who I was before."

Her brother put an arm around her shoulders and gave her a bracing hug. "Kira, do you remember when you were nine years old and our father brought you to taekkyon training with the saulabi for the first time? Father had been boasting about how good you were for days. It was not the best idea, and even he admitted it later on. All the boys were resentful and determined to put you in your place."

Kira nodded slowly. She'd been so intimidated by the mean remarks and nasty glares of the bigger boys that she had failed miserably in her first showing. She still remembered the mocking laughter that had followed her home that day.

"Do you remember what Father said to you?"

"He said that the only thing that can defeat me is my own fear," she replied.

"And what happened the following week when you came in for your real training?"

Kira smiled. "I showed them."

Her brother tapped her head lightly. "Yes, you did."

The next time she'd gone with her father, she'd been determined to prove herself. No one could touch her that day. She'd sent several of the older boys home with more than bruised egos.

"There's something very important that you have forgotten. It is not your tiger spirit that trained you to be a great saulabi, it was our father," he reminded her. "You do a grave disservice to his memory when you disregard his words and let fear rule you. Now try again."

Pride straightened her spine. What a fool she was! All those years of training with her father and brothers were what made her a warrior. Kyoung was right: she could not disrespect her father's memory. It didn't matter that she felt like a part of her had been ripped away. She was still General Kang's only daughter. That would never change.

She returned to the basics, as her father had always trained her to do. Go through her taekkyon forms. As she practiced, her muscle memory kicked in. This was what she'd trained to do all her life. This was second nature to her. By the end of their training session, Kira felt a return of hope, a sense of renewed energy.

The next day, they returned to the practice area. This

time her brothers brought a few soldiers. Kira recognized them as Kyoung's most trusted officers. Men who had trained with him under their father.

Her brother had his men attack in hand-to-hand combat. First two, then three, and then five at a time. Not holding back.

She leaped into the air and came down hard on two of the men. The other two she swept off their feet with a scissor kick. Jumping back onto her feet, Kira grappled the last man onto his stomach. It took less than a minute for her to overcome them.

Without wasting any time, Kwan stepped forward, facing her with a staff for sword practice. He was one of the saulabi's best swordsmen. He grinned wickedly at her.

"Been a long time since we had a go at each other, little sister," he said. "Come on then. Let's see how good you are now!"

As she took her fighter's stance, a rush of adrenaline coursed through her blood, heightening her senses. It felt good to spar with her brother. He knew her movements and habits as well as she knew his. There were no secrets or surprises. Only staffs clanging in a furious tempo as the two siblings tried to exploit potential weaknesses. Kyoung finally called a draw when the second set of staffs was cracked.

At the end of the day, they were all breathing hard, all except for Kira.

"What have we learned today, little sister?" Kyoung asked.

"It was not my tiger spirit that made me a strong fighter," she answered.

"So then, what have you lost?" Kyoung asked.

"I've lost my ability to sense demons," she said. "I can't see at night like I used to and I've lost my ability to heal from injury."

"So you can't see demons anymore, but can you still smell them?"

"I don't know," she said. Her sense of smell was still as acute as ever, but would it pick up the hidden demon odor?

"Now you can't see in the dark like a cat, but you can still see perfectly fine otherwise, right?"

Kira agreed.

"I think the most difficult thing you've lost is your ability to heal. I'd always envied you that. But this doesn't affect your fighting, right?"

She reluctantly agreed. "If I get hurt, I will recover slower."

"And you're still the best fighter I've ever seen," Kyoung said. "There's no one alive who can fight like you. Remember that."

"I can't jump as high as I used to. I'm not as strong either."

Kyoung tapped her on her nose. "That depends on your perspective. You still jump higher than any man, and you're stronger than most of these soldiers. Your special abilities were never of this world. They were gifts from the spirit world. You must now fight like a human, but you are still stronger, faster, smarter, and more agile than anyone I know. So what does this all mean?" he asked. "You can't see humans possessed by demons, but you still might be able to smell them. You can't see in the dark, but you can still see normally. And you will not be able to heal magically. I think you aren't in as bad a position as you might have thought. Do not doubt yourself."

"I miss my tiger spirit," she whispered. "I miss it so much."

"I am so sorry for that, but your tiger spirit sacrificed itself to save you," Kyoung said. "It is important that you not betray its memory. It is important that you do all in your power to prove to your tiger spirit that its sacrifice was worth it."

These words, more than any others, hit her hard. Her tiger spirit had sacrificed itself for Kira. She would not let its death be in vain. She might not be the Dragon Musado, but she was still her father's daughter. And she would have her vengeance.

There would be no stopping her.

20

She was standing in an empty throne room. Her body was completely rigid. She felt the invasive presence of the daimyo in her mind. She held a dagger in her left hand and her sword in the other. The dagger was long with a black, jagged blade and whispering demon voices. From the entranceway, Taejo raced in with Jindo, Major Pak, and a retinue of soldiers.

"Quick! Lock the doors and barricade them! We must protect the prince!" Major Pak said. Kira heard the howling and banging against the doors of a demon force eager to capture the prince.

Jindo began to bark and growl, warning them all of Kira's presence.

"Noona," Taejo called to her. "What are you doing standing there?"

When he tried to walk to her, Jindo ran in front of him, pushing him away. He continued to bark and growl.

Kira had not moved. Her body was rigid, but her arms rose up.

Taejo's eyes grew round with fright. Major Pak and his soldiers charged her. Kira dispatched them in short order. Cutting each soldier with the tip of the dagger, she watched as their bodies fell like blackened statues until only Major Pak and Jindo were left. The demons at the door had gone curiously quiet.

"Noona, you promised to protect me," Taejo shouted. "You must fight it!"

There was the slightest hesitation in her step as she tried valiantly to fight off the intruder. But the daimyo's viselike control tightened, causing her to fall down on one knee. Her head felt like it would explode in pain.

"Noona! You are fighting him! I can see that! Don't let him win! Noona, can you hear me? Please listen to me!"

The pain increased as blood vessels exploded in her eyes and her nose. But the daimyo forced her slowly up to her feet, her arms raised again. Major Pak attacked immediately, his double sword form pushing her back. Her body reacted in perfect defense, parrying his blows with ease. Her controlled mind took over as she swiftly stabbed him in the gut with her cursed dagger.

As his dying body turned a blackish gray, Jindo rushed forward and bit down hard on her left arm. The surprise of the bite caused the control to slip. She welcomed the ache and throbbing that brought her back to herself for a moment. Again she tested the control of the daimyo, looking to break the hold. But too soon, the daimyo paralyzed her mind. He controlled her sword arm, sending it thrusting down into the white dog's body. Taejo screamed and rushed forward, kneeling by his faithful companion's body. He looked up at her with eyes swimming with tears. He lifted his chin proudly and waited.

With a tremendous effort Kira wrestled with the vise inside her head. Her nose started to bleed but she forced herself to form two words.

"Run, please!"

Taejo shook his head sadly.

Her mind was screaming at him. Begging him to get away.

Kira could not stop the forward movement of her left arm. Tears wet her cheeks as she thrust the dagger through his abdomen and then caught his falling body. His eyes were still on hers as they dulled with pain.

"Noona," he whispered, and then he was gone.

It was the middle of the night when Kira woke from the nightmare, her whole body shivering in fright. Covering her head, she rocked back and forth, trying to shake off the vision.

Throwing off her covers, she got up on shaky legs and fled the room. Outside the house, she sat on the porch and let the cool night air clear her mind. The dark sky was cloudless and filled with stars. Kira stared up at the large full moon, and for a brief moment she wished she could fly far away to a place where she could never cause harm to those she loved.

Nothing had ever frightened her as much as these visions. They couldn't be true. She wouldn't let them come true. But how could she stop the daimyo from controlling her mind? It was inevitable that she would see him again. Kira knew this. The only way she would survive their encounter was if she could break his control. She analyzed the vision, remembering what she'd felt, those small countermovements that she was able to make against the daimyo's will.

She focused on the instances where she was able to speak or stop moving. What was it she'd done to cause a slight break in his control? If she focused on that, then she would have her answer. She had to look at these visions as a test. As horrifying as they were, they were sent to help her. She had to remember. Or else, she would fail.

She suddenly noticed that someone was in her courtyard. Jumping down from her porch, she walked over to the corner bench and found Jaewon curled up asleep. She stood watching him for a long moment. He looked so young and at peace.

A rush of affection filled her. She knelt by his side and brushed a gentle hand across his cheek.

"I've missed you," she said.

Jaewon stirred and then blinked his eyes open, pushing himself up. Kira sat next to him.

"I thought you were avoiding me this whole time, and then I find you in my courtyard," she said.

He was quiet. In his hands was a piece of wood and his small paring knife.

"The light's best here when it gets dark," he said. He pointed to the lit stone lantern that was next to the bench. "Your brother likes to keep that lit for you, just in case you want to come out at night."

"So you come here only for the light?"

There was no answer, only the sound of the scraping wood.

"Are you upset with me?"

No answer.

"Is it because you saw Shin Bo Hyun in my room?"

He nicked himself with his knife, cursing in pain. Seeing the blood welling up on his finger, Kira grabbed his hand to examine the wound. He tried to resist, but was stopped by her glare. She ran over to the barrel of water that sat on the porch and brought him a ladleful, pouring it over his cut. It was shallow and the bleeding stopped soon.

"There, it's not that bad," she said, smiling up at him.

Jaewon looked down at her with eyes filled with a sad longing. He gently pulled his hand away and stood up.

"I should go now."

"Kim Jaewon!" Kira yelled at him. "Don't you dare walk away from me!"

He stopped but didn't turn around. With an exasperated sigh, Kira walked in front of him, stabbing her finger into his chest.

"Where have you been when I've needed you? When I needed a friend! When I was at my darkest hour and suffering. Where were you?"

He gaped at her. "I tried to see you. Believe me, I did so many times, but your brothers wouldn't let me in."

"You should have sneaked in to see me, then."

"Oh you mean like Shin Bo Hyun did!"

"Yes, at least he came to see me!"

"He did a lot more than see you—"

"So you *were* there!"

"Yes." He pulled away. "And I saw you embracing and kissing him. I couldn't stand it."

"Wrong! You saw *him* embracing and kissing me. There's a big difference."

She stepped closer and wrapped her arms around Jaewon, resting her cheek against his shoulder. "The difference is I would never do this to Shin Bo Hyun."

Jaewon let out a hiccupping breath and hugged her tight.

"I told you that you held my heart," he whispered. "It's fragile and easily broken, but it's yours."

"Maybe I'm not worthy of it," she said.

"But you are. My world was dark before I met you. I lived every day without truly caring for what would come next. But now I have a purpose and a reason to look forward to every day. To see you, even if it is but for a moment."

Kira covered his lips with her hand, stopping the

flow of words. "I'm sorry I hurt you," she said. "I care for you so much. You're my best friend, and I'm so fortunate to have you in my life. Please don't forget that."

There was clear disappointment on his face at her words.

"Sometimes I can't help but wish for more," he said.

Kira shook her head. "That's all I can give right now."

There was a subtle withdrawing in Jaewon's manner that might not have been caught if Kira hadn't come to know him so well. He smiled, but his eyes seemed far away.

"I'll let you go back to sleep then," he said. "You need your rest."

She watched him walk out of the courtyard and felt the nagging sense of having made a terrible mistake. Something in her gut urged her to chase after him, but her feet wouldn't move. It was too late.

21

"We have word that the Second, Third, and Fifth Divisions are still a few days from reaching Asan," Kyoung said, speaking to Kira, Kwan, and Taejo. "Demon attacks are increasing on our patrols. We've lost squads of soldiers. The shamans are increasing the protective wards around us, but we must be vigilant once we're on the move. There's been no sign of General Kim and the Fifth Division, but I'm sure they're heading to Nosong as we speak. Since we are closer, it won't take us as long. We must mobilize the entire army. Everyone must prepare. We leave in two days."

"What can I do to help?" Taejo asked.

"Continue to train with me, little cousin," Kyoung

said. "You're making a great impression not only on your officers but also your soldiers. The officers are proud to see you at all the meetings, listening carefully and asking such intelligent questions, and your men are grateful when you walk among them. You are proving yourself a worthy king."

Kira was relieved to hear how Taejo had been spending his days. She'd felt guilty at pushing him away, but now she realized it was a good thing. He was becoming a man. He was becoming their king.

Preparing to move a vast army was always a tumultuous project. Both her brothers were too busy now to train with her, but she had her own preparations. Kira stayed out of the way, getting ready for the coming war in her own fashion. She thanked the women servants who had taken such good care of her. They'd made several new outfits for all of their party, to replace those that had become old and worn. This was especially helpful for Taejo, who had grown so much.

Kira repacked her old sack and then stayed in the privacy of her room. Her hand fluttered to her chest to where the tidal stone and her little haetae should have been. Her hand brushed against the silver dragon on its long chain.

"I fear that there will be more danger and heartache ahead for you. And you must stay strong, no matter how difficult it proves to be. No matter how beaten down you feel, you must not

give up. Rely on your strengths and have faith in yourself. No one else can do that but you."

The Dragon King had been right. But staying strong had been harder than Kira ever imagined. Her hand strayed lower to where a new tiny bag sat on her chest. She fingered the edges of the little tiger Jaewon had made her. Having lost her father's haetae, Jaewon's tiger had now become her solace, a reminder of the tiger spirit that she had loved so dearly. And while it could never replace the little haetae that her father had given her, the very fact that Jaewon had made it for her was reason alone to cherish it forever. She sighed deeply. Jaewon was avoiding her again. But this time she couldn't blame him and she didn't have anything to say that would help the situation.

There was a knock outside her room. When she opened the door, she found herself looking up into Shin Bo Hyun's face.

"Kang Kira, may I have a moment alone with you?" Shin asked.

"What is it?" she asked.

"I would prefer to talk to you somewhere else, if you don't mind," he said. "I don't want your brother catching me here alone with you. He still hates me and would need very little excuse to slit my throat."

"Don't exaggerate," Kira responded. "He's grateful for your presence and all of your men. He wouldn't hurt you."

Shin smirked at her. "I beg to differ. And he may not

need to kill me, only maim me a little."

Kira sighed. "There's a small backyard. No one will disturb us there. Follow me."

They walked the narrow hallways of the house and came out in the back, near the kitchens. The backyard had a henhouse and a garden. All the women servants had been sent to the magistrate's kitchens, where they were busy preparing food for the march.

Shin paced around the yard, a nervous bundle of energy.

"When the queen first told me about our betrothal, I was surprised but happy. I've always known that you were the only woman I could stomach the idea of marriage with. But I also knew how unhappy you were about our betrothal," he said. "It was something forced upon you by your aunt, the queen. And yet I couldn't help but hope that in time you would come around."

Kira listened to him with a growing sense of dread, unsure how to stop him.

"Then everything worsened with my traitorous uncle and his demands upon my fealty." Shin placed his hands on top of his head, a chagrined expression on his face. "Believe me, I know I've made a lot of mistakes. I was persuaded by my uncle that it was the right thing to do, but I should have known better."

He now stepped closer, facing Kira as he took hold of her hands.

"Times have changed and I have become a worthier

person. Even I like myself better now." He gave her his little side smile. "I think maybe you too have changed your feelings toward me. And although my uncle was a traitor, he was still the nephew to the king of Kudara. I am a cousin to the royal line and of noble blood. I am a good match for you, Kang Kira."

She pulled her hands away and placed distance between them, uncomfortably aware of his overwhelming masculine presence.

"Shin Bo Hyun," she started carefully. "I am sorry, but I don't feel the same way that you do."

"Are you sure?" he asked. "Because I feel a connection between us. And I know you feel it too. You are not unaffected by me."

He closed the distance between them again. "You get nervous around me. I make you uncomfortable, and I know why. I can see it in your eyes, Kira. They betray you every time." He lowered his head, capturing her lips with his, holding her firmly in his embrace. There was no mistaking his passion and the answering spark it lit within her. For a moment, she yielded to his kiss, forgetting everything, enjoying the emotions that were surging within her. But then she felt the outline of her little tiger figurine pressing between them, and her thoughts flew back to Jaewon.

She slipped her fingers between their lips and turned her face away. After a moment, he dropped his arms and stepped away.

"You do feel what's between us," he said. "Don't lie to me . . ."

"We can't have this discussion now," she said.

"This is the perfect time! Before you are committed down this path any further." He grasped her hands. "We could run away, just you and me."

"And do what? If the Demon Lord wins, we have no world to run away to—don't you understand? And what of the Dragon Fighters? You can't desert them!"

"You're right. I can't desert my soldiers. And you are destined to be our great hero. I know this. As much as I want to keep you safe, I realize you have a part to play in this history that we are making. But let me fight by your side! Let the world know that you belong to me," he said.

Kira shoved him hard.

"I don't belong to anyone!" Kira fumed. "I'm not a possession. Please don't treat me like one."

"Then let me belong to you," he pleaded. "I want to share my feelings for you with everyone. I want our betrothal to be announced from every temple in the Seven Kingdoms. I want the world to know that you and I are meant to be together."

There was a long pause as Kira stared into his handsome face. She saw his sincerity and the truth of how much she meant to him.

"Shin Bo Hyun," she said carefully. "I don't know if that's true."

She heard his sharp intake of breath.

"It's because of the village chief's son, isn't it," Shin said with a harsh growl. "He's unworthy of you! He's nothing but a glorified peasant! And from what I understand he was a vagabond, exiled from his own village for murdering his young brother—"

"Stop it! That's enough! You know nothing about him! Don't you dare judge him!"

In the sudden quiet, Kira glared at Shin, whose anger was clear in his flared nostrils and narrowed eyes.

"Please, Kira, don't mistake gratitude and friendship for something more," he said.

"Why not? That's all I feel toward you also," she retorted.

Shin reared back. His face closed up, looking harsh and angry, yet Kira could see the hurt in his eyes.

"My apologies. I will leave you alone then," he said with a bow.

"Shin Bo Hyun, I'm sorry if I hurt you," she said. "I do care for you very much."

Kira was suddenly mindful of these same words that she had said to Jaewon.

He put up a hand to stop her. "I understand," he said, his eyes cold and distant, a bitter smile curling his lip. "I shouldn't have expected anything more. Don't worry, Kang Kira, I won't bother you again."

With a curt bow, he walked away, leaving Kira feeling guilty and upset.

* * *

Several hours later, Kira went looking for Shin, hoping to clear the air between them. She was surprised to hear that he had joined the first scouting party of the day and had not come back yet. Suddenly anxious, Kira began to worry. When several more hours passed without any hint of their return, Kira asked to go search for them.

"Absolutely not," Kwan said. "I've already sent a few men after them. The last thing we need is you roaming around the countryside with the daimyo so near."

She knew he was right, but her concern for Shin was growing. She sensed that he was in trouble and needed help. But she didn't know what to do.

Late into the night, Kira had resorted to patrolling the perimeter of the city, hoping to see Shin's return. She heard the commotion of a new party returning to base camp. Kira made her way to the western gate, when a familiar but ugly stench hit her. She recognized it immediately as the rotten stink of demon. A rush of gratitude surged through her when she realized that she had not lost her sense of smell. Relieved and yet troubled, she followed her nose and found the sole survivor of the earlier scouting group.

Kira didn't want to believe her eyes. It was Shin Bo Hyun. A sob of grief wrenched out of her as she watched him being greeted by the Dragon Fighters, worried for their leader.

"Not Shin Bo Hyun," she breathed. She took out her

sword, tears beginning to fall. Slowly, she approached him.

As the Dragon Fighters led Shin back to their campsite, Kira blocked their path.

"What are you doing? Is this how you greet a friend after a long and dangerous mission?" Shin said. A nervous looked flashed over his face.

"Yes, you're right. He was my friend," she whispered. "I should've never let this happen to him."

"And I'm still your friend, returned safely to you," he said. He raised his hands and approached her cautiously. "Why are you so confused? I know that you've lost your magic tiger eyesight. Poor thing. When your eyes turned from yellow to brown, did you lose the capacity to distinguish friend from foe? Perhaps your eyesight has been more damaged than even you realize."

"I don't need my tiger eyes when you stink of demon!"

"Of course I do! I've been fighting them all day long! I barely escaped with my life! What else would I smell like?"

She wavered. Was she wrong? The smile on his face looked the same as always, but his eyes were flat and emotionless. And cold. So cold.

"You're acting so strange—are you sure you're all right?" he asked.

Kira's arm lowered. She wasn't sure.

"If anyone should be upset it should be me," he said. "Even knowing this betrothal was what your father wanted for us, you rejected me for another. An unworthy suitor!"

At his words, Kira's arms moved automatically, directing her sword at Shin's neck. His eyes widened as he leaped back, barely missing her attack. He drew his sword and gave an ugly grimace, unlike anything she'd ever seen on his face. Kira was glad she no longer had the ability to see the demon underneath the human skin. It would have been too hard to see it overtake the face of her friend.

The Dragon Fighters drew their swords, determined to protect their leader.

"My lady!" a captain of the Dragon Fighters shouted. "Please back away! We cannot let you harm our commander."

"But that's the problem," she said. "He's not your commander. And he's not my friend either. That is not Shin Bo Hyun!"

Someone called for her brother Kwan as the Iron Army soldiers also drew their swords.

"Do you realize how crazy you sound?" Shin asked. "It's me! Lord Shin! Your former betrothed! How can you not know me?"

"My father never approved of him," she said in a hard undertone. "And Shin Bo Hyun knew that."

Shin's men had been circling them and drew back at her words, lowering their swords in confusion.

"How would I know that? Maybe this is something

your father told you in secret!" Shin blustered, his eyes shooting from left to right.

"Shin Bo Hyun would know this," she said. "Because I told him."

"I fear your memory is at fault," he said. "You only think you told me. This is all because you have lost your powers. You are not in your right mind, my dear. Someone take her sword away before she does something she'll regret."

No one moved. It was a frozen tableau of indecision and danger. Kira swiped at the tears that kept leaking from her eyes.

"If you are truly Shin Bo Hyun, you would have his full memory. But if you are a demon, you would only have knowledge of his most recent memories. So, what did Shin Bo Hyun tell me right before he left me in the Yalu River?" she asked.

"How am I supposed to remember this? You are unreasonable!"

"It was something Shin Bo Hyun wanted me to remember. Now what was it?"

"I don't know!"

Furious, he attacked her. Kira held off his driving blows, their fight scattering his men as their swords clashed hard. A sudden calm came over her. She knew now what she had to do. With a swift move, she deflected his blow. Then, grabbing her dagger with her left hand, she spun around and stabbed him in the throat.

He fell to the ground as black ooze began to seep out of the jagged wound and Shin's body began to deflate.

Kira collapsed onto her knees next to what was now just skin and bones within Shin's uniform. The tears rolled down her face as she remembered his long-ago words.

"I told you I would do anything for you," Shin said. She could feel his finger running down the side of her cheek and see his sideways smile. "It was good to see you again, Kira."

"I'm sorry, Shin Bo Hyun!" Kira wept. "This was my fault. You shouldn't have left me in anger. I shouldn't have let you leave."

Kwan knelt by her side, pulling her away from the macabre corpse. "It wasn't your fault, Kira," he said. "The evil done here was by the daimyo and the Demon Lord. You are not to blame. Kira? Are you listening to me?"

The hurt and guilt cut deep. If only she hadn't driven him away, would he still be here by her side? Did she do wrong in turning him down? Should she have given him hope?

Despite all their differences, he'd become a friend, one whom she trusted deeply, one who had sacrificed himself numerous times for her. She wished he'd never come back into her life. Chansu was right. She was the reason Shin was dead.

It hurt her to know that this time she would never see him again.

22

"Young mistress," a servant called to her from outside her door. "There are a group of soldiers here to see you. They say it is urgent."

With a tired sigh, Kira rose to her feet. She'd become too used to sleeping. Inertia and depression threatened to constantly overtake her.

Late in the night, Jaewon had knocked softly at her door, asking her if she was all right. When she didn't answer, he'd said, "I'm sorry about Shin Bo Hyun. He was a great soldier and devoted to you. As jealous as I was, I would not have wished this on him."

After he left, Kira held tightly to her little tiger

figurine and tried not to cry anymore.

Outside her room, she pulled on her boots and exited the house. As she stepped onto the patio that led to the courtyard, she paused at the incredible sight before her. All of Shin Bo Hyun's army stood before her, numbering over a hundred men and women.

"What are you doing here?" she asked.

A female soldier stepped forward and bowed. "I am Ha Minhee. I was first captain under Major Lee and Commander Shin. With the death of the major and our commander, I am currently in charge of the Dragon Fighters," she said. "We want to stay and fight, but the Dragon Fighters are now leaderless. We cannot be absorbed into another battalion. We're not professional soldiers. What we do best is guerrilla warfare. And we need a leader who understands us. And more than a third of our force are women fighters. You're the only female to have ever been accepted into an official army. You're one of the elite saulabis. That's why we're here. The Dragon Fighters would like to ask you to be our leader."

Kira couldn't speak at first, fighting to retain her composure. She was so touched by the display of faith they showed in her.

"I am deeply honored by your request," she said. "But are you sure about this? I'm no longer the same person I was before." Her voice grew hoarse. She cleared her throat. "Perhaps my second brother would be the wiser choice."

Captain Ha shook her head. "You are our only choice. And we believe it was what our commander would have wanted."

Kira had to look away. She refused to cry anymore. The sharp pain of Shin's loss was too recent. The guilt too hard to overcome. But perhaps this was what he would have wanted. Maybe by taking over this group of soldiers that he had become so close to, she could honor his memory in some way.

"Captain Ha, if you would be my first in command, then I would be happy to be your leader," she said.

The Dragon Fighters cheered, setting off a loud roar.

Kira stood on the raised porch of the house she'd hidden herself away in. For the first time since losing her tiger spirit, she felt a renewed energy and purpose.

"Shin Bo Hyun," she whispered, "I shall lead your soldiers into battle and we will seek a victory in your honor. I promise."

"Noona," Taejo called to her. "I must speak with you privately."

Kira opened the door and let her cousin into her room. They sat on opposite sides of the room, leaning comfortably against the walls.

"I feel guilty that I was never nice to Shin Bo Hyun," Taejo said. "And now it's too late to apologize to him for all that he did to help us."

"I'm sorry too for being the one to drive him away," Kira said. "But I think he knew. He knew we needed him and appreciated his help. It was not in his nature to stay where he wasn't wanted or needed."

"So Sunim was right. He really was a good man," Taejo said.

"Yes, he was. He redeemed himself from all that his uncle had done and forced him to do. He died a hero," Kira said.

The silence between them was heavyhearted.

"Noona, I'm frightened."

Taejo hung his head, looking ashamed of the words he'd uttered. "I've been having terrible nightmares," he whispered. "Filled with monsters that are overtaking the world. And life as we know it is no more. But the scariest dream I had was the one with you."

He hesitated, his eyes round and frightened.

"It's all right, tell me," she said.

Taking a deep breath, he spoke quickly, his words jumbling together in his rush. "I dreamed that you were under the control of the daimyo and were trying to kill me."

Kira bolted up, shuddering at the vision that came instantly to mind. This was not a coincidence. Her worst fear could possibly come true. Kira's heart pounded in her chest as if she'd been running up a mountain. A fear like never before iced over her spine.

"Listen to me," she said urgently. "You must promise me that if I ever appear as if I'm not in control of myself, you are to run away from me—do you understand?"

He looked more frightened. "Why are you saying this?"

Running a frantic hand through her short locks, Kira took a deep breath and calmed herself, willing her racing heart to slow down.

"I have had the same dream," she said. "It is a vision. You know my visions. They tend to come true. But this one scares me to death too."

She crawled over to his side and sat cross-legged before him. "Promise me that you will run from me if that ever happens."

He hesitated and shook his head. "I can't promise that."

"You must!" she said. "If I'm under the control of the daimyo, you have only two choices. You must either kill me or run away from me. I fear that you will not be able to kill me. Therefore you must do whatever it takes to save yourself. Swear this now!"

He nodded slowly. "I promise to save myself."

Only then did Kira subside. But the coldness in her heart stayed in place. She walked him to his room on the other side of the house and left him in Brother Woojin's company. She turned to Gom, stroking the little dokkaebi's wiry hair.

"Gom, I need you to stay by the prince's side at all times," she said. "And if you ever see me try to attack him, you must stop me. That is an order."

Gom's face looked confused and sad. "It's all right, Gom." She hugged him close for a moment. "Don't be sad. But I'm afraid of what will happen if the daimyo gets control of me. I need to know you will protect the prince, even from me, OK? This is the right thing to do. I promise. But, please, stay with the prince."

The dokkaebi sat in front of the prince's door, looking forlorn. It was hard for Kira to leave him, but she knew he would protect Taejo.

She then went off to find her brothers. They were pouring over maps and charts in the command center. Nostalgia hit her. She remembered when she would walk into the supreme commander's office and see her brothers standing beside their father. She could see her father's stern face lighten into a smile at her entrance. She missed him so much.

They looked up at her expectantly. Kira swallowed down the bile that had suddenly risen in her throat. This would not be an easy conversation to have.

"I need to tell you something important," she said. "Something I know will come true because I have had many visions of it. I'm afraid the daimyo will be able to control me."

"Why? What makes you say that?" Kyoung asked.

With a deep breath Kira explained her visions; she told of the first where she had killed her brothers, then of the more recent one where she attacked Taejo.

"Taejo has never had a vision before, but suddenly he is having dreams where I'm under the control of the enemy? This is not a coincidence," she said.

"But it might also be a vision of what the daimyo

wants us to believe," Kwan said. "Maybe he is manipulating your dreams."

Kira shook her head. "No, I know the difference between a vision and a dream. I also know what it feels like to have someone in your head manipulating you. These visions are telling us what might happen and we have to listen. We must be ready for it.

"You must do what you have to do to stop me," she said grimly.

"We need to keep you from the daimyo," Kwan said.

Kira disagreed. "That is not the answer," she said. "My fight is with the daimyo. I must face him. And I must stop him from controlling me. But if I lose . . ."

They looked at her with agonized expressions.

"No," Kwan said. "There must be another way."

"You must both promise me that you will kill me if you cannot stop me," Kira said. "Promise me! If anything were to happen to either of you or Taejo or—" Kira caught herself from saying Jaewon's name "—or anyone else I care about, I would not be able to live with myself. You must understand that."

Kyoung pulled her into a tight embrace, while Kwan placed a hand on the back of her head. They stood together like this for a long time.

"Promise me . . ."

They nodded and hugged her tight.

23

On the morning of their departure for Nosong, Taejo called a meeting of the generals. All three of the Kang siblings were there, as was Major Pak.

"I want to lead my men into battle," Taejo said. "I want them to know that they can count on me to be there for them."

The generals looked uneasy, but Kyoung beamed proudly at Taejo. "The saulabi have been waiting for you, Your Highness. My brother and Major Pak will flank you and be your first and second in commands. Kira and the Dragon Fighters will join your formation. Your father would be proud."

Kira was amazed to see that Taejo was as tall as most of the generals in the room. He wore his bright silver armor well, carrying his helmet at his side. He had grown so quickly. Almost thirteen years old and ready to lead an army into battle. Was he really ready? Would he be safe?

She sent her brother a concerned look.

He gazed back at her steadily.

"The prince must show his people that he is ready to be a king," he said. "This is his chance for glory. We must all support him."

As everyone agreed, Kyoung continued. "This is also your moment, little sister. The prophecy has always been about you, not the prince. I think we all recognize this now. Even Brother Woojin has agreed that the interpretation of the monks was false. The One of the prophecy is you and only you. You must now meet your destiny without the shackles placed on you by our uncle and our father in their efforts to protect the prince. You've met those vows. Now, you must let him go and fulfill your role in the prophecy. Are you ready?"

Kira exhaled a long, drawn-out breath that released the last of her self-doubts.

"Yes, I am."

"Then let's go kill the daimyo and drive this demon scum off our land!"

They left for Nosong immediately. Kira joined the Dragon Fighters, adding their distinctive headband to her forehead.

Her hair had grown long enough to pull into a stubby ponytail. Nara rode by her side, changed back into a Dragon Fighter's uniform of red.

But it was the sight of Jaewon that shocked Kira the most. When she saw him, she caught her breath. He'd changed into full armored gear to match her own. He wore a black saulabi uniform under the black-scaled armor that covered his entire torso. Leather bracers protected his forearms while the Dragon Fighters' insignia was displayed proudly on his forehead. His long hair was left flowing down his back instead of tied up into a topknot like the others. He looked amazing. She noticed the admiring looks he was getting from the female soldiers. Kira felt a fluttering inside her chest as he approached her.

"You look good," she said gruffly.

He gave her an admiring look. "So do you."

Seung rode with him. He too was wearing a headband and leather armor. His friendly face seemed untroubled by the danger they were heading into.

"Look, they have given me a sword," Seung said in awe. "I've never had my own before."

"I thought you were going to stay in the medical tent," Kira said in confusion.

Seung nodded solemnly. "Your brother said just in case, I should have a sword."

Understanding dawned. "Then I hope that you will never have to use it," she said.

Their group joined with Taejo, who was flanked by Kwan and Major Pak. Brother Woojin rode behind them and Jindo and Gom kept up on foot.

As they rode, Jaewon stayed close to Kira.

"I don't know what will happen in Nosong. But I wanted to tell you that I regret nothing," Jaewon said.

"Me too," Kira said.

"Maybe one day, we can go back to Modo Island and walk across that bridge without worrying about drowning," he said.

"Only if we get to eat Grandma Song's grilled fish and soy sauce eggs again," Kira replied.

Jaewon groaned. "Why did you have to remind me! My mouth is watering."

They laughed as they traded their memories of happy times.

"When I first saw you in the stables that night we met, I thought you were like someone out of my dreams," he said.

"More like nightmares, you mean," she quipped.

"No, Kira. I've always thought you were the most beautiful girl in the world," he said.

Kira was silent. "Do you still feel that way even though my eyes are plain old brown?" she asked.

"Plain old brown?" he asked in amazement. "If that is what you call them, you have not really looked at them."

It was true that Kira had been avoiding mirrors, even more so than ever before. The one time she looked, she'd hardly recognized herself. Most of the self-inflicted scratches had faded away but for one claw mark that had gouged the middle of her cheek. The same cheek that had been marred by the whip so long ago. Her eyes were so dark now that she almost felt like she was looking at another person.

"Before your eyes were a golden yellow, now they are a golden brown. To be honest, I can't really describe them. I think they are beautiful," he said.

A light rosy flush covered Kira's cheeks. She was still not used to anyone calling her beautiful. Self-conscious, she rubbed her fingers along her old and new scars. Jae-won reached over and pulled at a curl that had come loose.

"Do you remember that night on Modo when you slept in my arms?" he asked.

"I'd had a terrible nightmare," she said.

He nodded, smiling, with a faraway look on his face. "That was the happiest night of my life," he said. "Because I got to hold you and watch you sleep."

Kira was moved, a lump forming in her throat at the wistfulness in his voice. "Don't let my brother hear you," she warned in a husky voice.

"I wouldn't tell anyone," he said. "I refuse to share that memory. It is precious to me."

"Me too," Kira replied.

Suddenly, a horse maneuvered in between them, forcing them apart. Kwan glared at Jaewon and then at Kira. "I think I will ride with my sister for some time," he said.

Jaewon agreed with a slight inclination of his head and rode ahead to join Seung. Kira smiled at him as he passed before meeting her brother's indignant gaze.

"I thought you used to like him," Kira said with a reproachful look.

"I do like him, which is why he's not dead yet," Kwan retorted. "And he'd better not touch you again before your betrothal is announced."

Kira huffed. "I didn't say anything about a betrothal."

"Well then he'd better not touch you again or there *will* be a betrothal. That or a funeral. I will be happy with either outcome."

The journey to their battle position was uneventful. They passed two forts and a few villages. All of them abandoned, all of them completely destroyed by the Yamato. Fear crept into Kira. The last time they had come upon abandoned villages, they'd been attacked by an army of demon-possessed humans. She worried that this would be the case again.

Kira spent the rest of the journey getting to know Captain Ha and the Dragon Fighters better. They reminisced about Shin Bo Hyun and told stories about his exploits.

"He talked about you a lot," Captain Ha said. "How you were the most amazing woman he'd ever met. And how he hoped that one day you'd forgive him all the wrongs he had done."

Kira swallowed the lump in her throat. "I did," she said. "I came to think of him as a friend."

She let out a small sad laugh. "I used to hate him so much when we were younger," she said. "He was always trying to get me in trouble. Or so I thought. But now I realize, it was just his way of being around me." She wiped away a tear that had leaked out of the corner of her eye. "I'm learning about perspective, you know? How you never really know the answer to something unless you can look at it from all the different sides. I wish I'd had some more time with him. I wish I'd told him that I forgave him for everything."

Captain Ha looked up to the skies. "I'm sure he knows now," she said.

They reached their destination in the early afternoon of the third day. The warm spring weather had been perfect for journeying. Reconnaissance showed them that they were not the first division to arrive. The scouts came back with four thousand members of the rebel forces from the Fifth Division, General Kim's command. Most of the soldiers looked shaken up. Whispers of demons and inhumanity swept the troops. Kira, Kwan, and Taejo, along with the rest of their party, made their way to Kyoung's side to discover what had happened.

They set up camp below a long, wide ridge that circled and overlooked the plains outside Nosong. Kyoung ordered Kwan and Kira to follow him, leaving the rest to stay in the quickly forming tent that would make up their command center. Kwan and Kira followed their brother up the ridge to peer at the enemy lines.

The plains of Nosong were filled with legions of Kudara and Yamato soldiers. There were at least fifty thousand men, of which Kira had no idea how many were demons and half-breeds. A soldier, in the red and black Kudara uniform, rode back and forth holding a long spear. What looked like a head was mounted on the end of the spear.

"Who is that?" Kira asked.

"General Kim," her brother answered. "Apparently he arrived before any of the other divisions. He decided he wanted to attack immediately. His unit leaders warned him it would be suicide, but he didn't listen. The guerrilla units refused to join him. He led a vanguard of five thousand men into Nosong before anyone could stop him. They were slaughtered."

It was a sobering reality. As much as Kira disliked the old general, it was wrong to see his head treated with such little respect. In the field before the Yamato camp, there was a large mound that was as wide as a small hut and nearly as tall as a tree.

"What is that mound over there?" she asked.

"The Yamato have made a mountain out of the cutoff heads of the men they killed," Kyoung continued. "They call them their trophies. Those were all General Kim's men."

Sickened, Kira had to look away.

"I wonder why they didn't possess them?"

"Maybe there are more bodies than demons," Kwan said.

"Or maybe they are trying to demoralize our men," Kyoung responded. "It worked on the rebel forces."

That made more sense to Kira. It was in keeping with how cruel the daimyo was that he would do something so evil and disturbing. Even from the distance, they saw the living cloud of flies that surrounded the macabre scene. She noticed that the Kudara camp seemed a good distance from the gruesome memorial. Perhaps not all of them approved of the daimyo's ways.

Returning to the command tent, Kyoung reported back to the others on what they had seen.

"If anything, you must use this to embolden our soldiers even more," Major Pak said. "To warn them that these are the stakes for us all."

A small unit of officers approached them. Kira recognized Lord Rah, the Oakcho ambassador; General Nam, the Guru minister of military affairs; and Lord Hwang, the Guru minister of foreign affairs who had helped them escape from Hansong.

"General Kang, the Third Division is in place and ready for your command," General Nam said.

"As is the Fourth Division, although I am sorry to report the death of Prince Namhoe of Tongey in a recent skirmish on our way to Asan," Lord Rah said.

"Who has assumed command of the Fourth?" Kyoung asked.

"I have," Lord Rah said.

"He was the best choice, Your Honor," Lord Hwang interjected. "As a former general of the Oakcho army and unaffiliated with Guru, he was the only choice that the Tongey would accept. And he has done an excellent job."

"Thank you, Lord Rah, for your quick thinking and command of the situation," Kyoung said. "I would like you to continue to lead the Fourth Division as a commanding general of the Iron Army."

"It would be my great honor," Lord Rah said with a deep bow.

"Then it is official: you are now an Iron Army general of Guru and serve the crown prince Taejo, King Eojin's heir."

The new general bowed deeply to Taejo. "I solemnly swear to honor and serve the rightful heir to the throne of Guru, and defend our prince and kingdom on pain of my life."

"Thank you, General Rah," Taejo said with deep sincerity. "You honor us all today."

He turned to the other officers with a welcoming nod. "Words cannot express my deep admiration and gratitude to all of you. Against all odds, you have led your men to this point. We now are faced with one final battle. Today will be a great day in the history of our country. I am honored to fight alongside you."

Kira had stood off to the side, watching the drama unfold. She was proud of her cousin—the boy who would be king. She saw the respect and approval for their young prince in the eyes of all the officers. She knew that they would fight for him and give their lives in service. Taejo was proving himself to be worthy of their uncle's throne.

It was decided that Brother Woojin and Seung would stay behind in medical tents, where they would both be the greatest help. And it was Taejo himself that decided to leave Jindo with them, tied to a tree. He whined and whimpered and kicked up a big fuss, but Taejo remained strong.

"No, Jindo, if you got hurt again, I would never forgive myself," he said. "Stay here and be a good boy! I promise I'll come back for you."

Kira patted Jindo and whispered, "Don't worry, I'll make sure Gom never leaves his side."

They left quickly and joined their soldiers. Major Pak and Kwan were mounted before the saulabi and Hansong army, a mix of black and white or silver uniforms. Off to their side, the Dragon Fighters were a vivid splash of vibrant and different colored vests over their black or white uniforms. Only their distinctive headbands unified them.

As they approached, Major Pak asked them to address their soldiers. Taejo went to the head of the Second Division. His young boy's voice had deepened and he spoke with an authority that belied his years. He spoke briefly but eloquently, thanking them all for their support and promising to lead them to victory. When the cheers died down, the Dragon Fighters looked to Kira.

Captain Ha yelled out, "Commander Kang, will you address your Dragon Fighters?"

Kira was surprised but pleased. Taking a deep breath, she began her speech.

"I am not much for making pretty speeches. I tend to leave the speechifying to my oldest brother." The Dragon Fighters chuckled at her wry expression. Kira noticed that the rest of the Second Division soldiers had now quieted down and were listening intently to her words.

"But maybe for the first time in my life, I have a burning inside me that seems to have freed my words. Today, I am honored and privileged to lead this brave group of warriors. While I wish Commander Shin was still here with us, I will do my best to be worthy of his place.

"Right now, we are faced with the biggest battle of our lives. The Demon Lord seeks to destroy our world by releasing the demon hordes and all the evil locked away in the underworld. He would enslave our people. This beautiful land would be gone and all that would be left is a hellhole. If you are afraid, know that you are not alone. I am afraid too. But not of dying! Never of dying. The only fear I have is that of losing. For losing is not an option, my friends.

"We must fight for our world. We must fight for our people. And we must be willing to die so that we can all live. In this coming battle, I see before us only two choices: fight for victory or lie down and die. And I do not plan to die today!"

A loud roar arose from the Dragon Fighters.

"Brothers and sisters, we will fight shoulder to shoulder with our fellow soldiers. Individually we may fall, but united we will prevail! We will take down each enemy one by one, we will win back our land step by step, and we will drive these demon scum back into the deepest darkest hell from which they came!"

The cheers of the soldiers was deafening. They began to chant "Demon Slayer" over and over as they marched up the ridge.

Kira grinned. For the first time ever, what had always been a pejorative term for her was now a source of power, one that soon raced across all the divisions of the Iron Army to become a rallying cry.

Now she was the Demon Slayer. She was ready.

The Kang siblings and Prince Taejo stood on the ridge overlooking the plains. The First and Second Divisions kept to the ridge below them, waiting their command. On the northern ridge, the Third and Fourth Division officers held their positions. The soldiers were still chanting "Demon Slayer" when the officers waved for quiet. They watched and waited as the Kudara and Yamato forces acknowledged them.

Four large barrel-shaped war drums were carried out to the front lines by eight red-uniformed Kudara soldiers. Soon drumbeats began to boom across the plains.

The repetitive drumming was an infectious call to

arms. Their soldiers banged their spears into the ground and against their shields. Louder and louder they got until they let off a sheer cacophony of noise.

The Iron Army's response began with a piercing whistle. Then they marched up the ridge and over it as their drummers began a strong but steady beat, countering the Kudara's. It built to a crescendo as the soldiers picked up the beat, banging their spears, shields, swords, and armor in time. More and more of the Iron Army and its allies marched over the ridge, beating their weapons until the sound swallowed up the noise from over the plains. The Kudara stared at the massed armies before them.

As the Iron Army's drums grew louder, more drummers appeared. The Second Division once again chanted "Demon Slayer" along with the pounding rhythm. Their battle cry caught quickly with the other armies. As the massive Iron Army and its allies marched over the ridge and into the plains, the drums and the chanting sent the enemy into disturbed chaos. By the time they stopped marching, the enemy was silent. Before them was a force of well over one hundred thousand men. When King Eojin had marched down from Guru, he had commanded an army of the same size. After their victory in Wonsan, he'd split the army, taking half to Hansong while the other half swept down the eastern coast and chased away all of the Yamato. Although they'd lost a lot of men in the battles, they'd picked up more volunteers and more displaced soldiers from the other kingdoms. Now the unified Iron Army was bigger than ever before.

Their infantry and cavalry was more than double the size of the enemy's.

"Look at them! They're scared," Jaewon said with a satisfied chuckle. "I bet they're gonna run!"

Kira eyed him and shook her head. "Do not underestimate the daimyo," she said.

Mounted officers raced in front of the vanguard, preparing them for battle. The drums quieted and the fields were silent except for the cries of the officers. All was still until Kyoung raised his arm and gave the signal. The drums began a fierce beating and ten thousand bowmen stepped forward. Kyoung bellowed and the vanguard of infantrymen charged forward. The bowmen sent off a hailstorm of arrows on the enemy. After the first wave of arrows, ten thousand more bowmen stepped forward and let loose another wave of arrows. Each group firing until the vanguard clashed with the enemy.

The enemy was already in disarray, showing a severe crack in their formation.

"Calvary forward!" Kyoung shouted.

Kira led the Dragon Fighters into battle, while Taejo and Kwan led the saulabi. All the cavalry descended upon the infantrymen. It was a bloodbath. Within minutes, the cavalry were past the enemy front lines and making short work of the Kudara and Yamato soldiers.

The enemy was now in full retreat. With a wild

deafening roar, the cavalry gave chase, cutting down the retreating men. Now that they were within enemy territory, Kira's sole mission was to find the daimyo. Her nose led her through the tangle of tents toward the southwest corner, where she spotted a large black structure. It was unlike any building she'd ever seen. The wooden beams that it was made from were pitch-black, as if painted and lacquered over for dramatic effect. There were no windows, only a small door with no visible latch. She was almost overwhelmed by the stench of demon magic it exuded.

"There he is," she said. She signaled the location to the others and called over her first in command.

"Captain Ha," Kira said, "I need half of our men on foot while I seek out the daimyo. You will take the rest and hold this perimeter."

The captain gave a curt nod and led half the guerrilla fighters to form a large perimeter around the black structure. As the others dismounted, Kira turned to Taejo and her brother Kwan.

"We will keep this area secure," Taejo said.

Kwan and Major Pak agreed. Even knowing that they would keep Taejo as safe as possible, Kira felt a pang of worry.

"Dokkaebi army!" Kira shouted. Immediately the dokkaebis appeared, some one hundred of them. "Protect the prince no matter what."

"And you," Kwan said sharply.

Kira stared at him.

Kwan waved her protest off. "You need to be protected too. Don't argue with me. Half with the prince, half with you. Agreed?"

Kira nodded.

"Good luck," Taejo said.

"You too," she replied.

Taejo led the saulabis to secure the perimeter. Meanwhile, Kira led her fighters to the edge of the forest nearby. They dismounted and left their horses.

As Kira led her unit toward the black building, her nose was assaulted by the overwhelming stench of demon.

"Demon attack!" she shouted, preparing for the onslaught.

Hundreds of half-breeds poured out of the tents that stood between them and the black building. Before they reached Kira and her soldiers, the dokkaebis appeared, whipping their cudgels so hard they were smashing half-breeds into the air. Even as this first pairing clashed, the thundering approach of more troops brought the Second Division infantry screaming into the mix. So thick were the bodies that Kira's unit had to move around the perimeter of the battle to approach the black building.

And then amid the chaos, the ground rumbled and a huge tremor shook them all. In the middle of the plains, a large crack formed across the battleground. From deep underground a massive imoogi erupted, bigger than any Kira had ever seen before. It scattered both armies and killed indiscriminately.

Upon sighting the imoogi, Kira and the Dragon Fighters stood in stunned surprise.

"Heavenly Father save us! How are we to fight that?" Jaewon said.

Nara was agitated. "How arrogant! He has appeared in the human world, against all laws of nature," Nara said.

"What do you mean?" Kira asked.

"The Demon Lord!" she spat out. "He has taken an earthly form. Kill the imoogi and the Demon Lord will be destroyed forever."

Kira stared at the imoogi. The Iron Army was in full attack, but with a sweep of its tail and a bite of its savage jaws, it was slowly destroying their advantage.

"We need help," she said. "Dokkaebi army!" She called out. Within seconds the dokkaebis appeared, Gom in the lead, bringing them to her. With a happy grunt, he disappeared again, returning to the prince's side.

"Dokkaebis!" Kira shouted. "There is the enemy. Destroy the imoogi!"

They surged as one across the plains and toward the imoogi. They pounded and bashed and ripped at flesh in an all-out attack. But a swoosh of its tail crushed many in one movement. And yet the dokkaebis pounded the imoogi with their cudgels and bit it with their mouths. The monster screamed in fury, its tail lashing at its tormentors, while its massive jaws snapped at them. But the dokkaebis had become wise to the imoogi's movements and now avoided them with ease.

"Now we must find the daimyo," Kira said grimly.

They trekked across the remains of the once proud Kudara command central. The tents had been trampled as the fighting raged around them. All that was left was the black building.

"He has to be there," Nara said. "He must stay near the imoogi to keep it in this world."

From around the corner, a large group of half-breed soldiers and demon-possessed humans descended upon them. While only Kira could detect their scent, anyone could see what they really were. They had been in their host bodies for too long and the rotted flesh had worn through, showing the demon underneath. It was a revolting sight.

This time Kira led the Dragon Fighters into a frontal assault. The battle had narrowed to this point of immediacy. Sword met sword as the half-breeds howled at them like the monsters they were. They clashed hard, Kira's soldiers quickly overwhelming the half-breeds. But within minutes, more appeared.

"Where are they all coming from?" Jaewon asked.

"The daimyo!" Kira knew this must be the army left to protect the daimyo. They had to be close.

Before they could be overtaken, Taejo's saulabis attacked. Kira saw Kwan and Major Pak, cutting down half-breeds from atop their horses. She spotted Taejo ordering his men, yet staying within their protection, as he'd promised. It took her a great force of will to leave him, but she had to find the daimyo and end all this.

She ran past the battle and around the destroyed Kudara communication centers. Not far away, she met with a squad of ten frightened Kudara soldiers.

"We surrender!" their commanding officer yelled. "He's turning my men into demons! This is not what we agreed to! We don't protect demons!"

"Then fight with us!" Kira commanded.

They agreed immediately, swearing fealty to Taejo. The Dragon Fighters made the Kudara soldiers take off their distinctive red helmets and tie on the dragon headbands.

Kira grinned. "Now we won't kill you accidentally. Where's the daimyo?"

They pointed to the black structure.

"Watch out," the Kudara officer said grimly. "There are more demon soldiers surrounding him. He seems to have an unending supply."

Even with ten more added to her group, Kira realized it was not enough. She called for a few dokkaebis to join her and Taejo. At her call, twenty of them broke off from the imoogi.

Captain Ha and the rest of the Dragon Fighters were now back. Kira sent them toward the daimyo's building, instructing them to circle around from the right. She sent the Kudara men to attack from the left. She took the straightest course.

Behind them, every division of the Iron Army still fought with the half-breed army. Though she heard the roars of the men and dokkaebis fighting the imoogi, she refused to look. She couldn't help any of them right now. She had to focus on the daimyo.

King Eojin's blackened and fearsome countenance suddenly sprung into her mind.

"The longer I stay in the shadow world, the more like a demon I become. If you don't save me, then I will become a full demon and it will be too late. . . . Remember your promise, Niece. Remember me."

Grim determination settled within her. For King Eojin and for Taejo, she would destroy the daimyo.

From within the smaller tents, demon soldiers continued their attack. It was immediately apparent they were newly demon-possessed bodies of what had once been Kudara soldiers. Kira recalled some of her dokkaebis, and a small group of them appeared, attacking immediately, stunning the demons by smashing them senseless.

"You must aim for the neck!" Kira called out, as she slashed and stabbed, leaving a trail of disintegrating bodies behind her. The dokkaebis and human army made a great partnership. Soon they reached the black structure, where more half-breeds and demons poured out.

Just then, paralysis gripped her. She froze in place.

"Kira, what's going on?" Jaewon asked.

She couldn't answer, her eyes trying to signal frantically of the coming danger. Jaewon turned to find half-breeds surrounding them.

Why do you fight me so hard? Aren't you tired? Now that

your tiger spirit is gone, you are nothing but a mere human girl.

She heard the voice of the daimyo speaking to her. His insidious thoughts filled her with doubt and self-hatred.

You are the reason for all that has happened. So much death. So much destruction. All because of you.

Visions of her mother and father and even her aunt flitted through her mind as an overwhelming guilt threatened to crush her.

Nobody cares about you. No one loves you. Come to me. Be my hero and we will crush this world like the insects that they are. Where is the jade belt? Let us release the dragons, Musado, and the world will be yours to command!

"Noona!" Kira heard Taejo's voice. He and the saulabis were now on foot, fighting the never-ending horde of half-breeds. What was Taejo doing there? She spotted Gom nearby waving his cudgel frantically at her.

"Noona! You must fight him!"

Kira saw the frightened eyes of her brother Kwan. His shaking hand moved to his bow, aware of what he must do if she was unable to break the daimyo's hold on her.

"Kim Jaewon!" Taejo yelled. "You have to get Noona away from here!"

Jaewon and the Dragon Fighters managed to break free of the half-breeds and began to run to Kira, when suddenly a wall of fire surrounded her.

Then the black structure exploded into flames, and a figure stepped out from the inferno. The daimyo had finally shown himself. As saulabis tried to attack him, the daimyo shot lightning from his fingertips, electrocuting the soldiers. From behind Kira, bowmen let loose their arrows at the daimyo. But each missile fell harmlessly before him, never reaching their target.

This is perfect. The princeling to be killed and the Dragon Musado to be taken. Thank you for making this all so easy for me and my master.

Taejo was now racing around Kira's flaming figure. "Noona!" he shouted again. "You have to fight him! Remember who you are!"

Kira caught sight of the gleam of the daimyo's dagger blade as he stepped with slow and deliberate intent toward them. She forced herself to clench and unclench her fist, putting all her energy into that one small act.

No one understands you. You were not meant to be with these pathetic creatures. Come to us and we shall make sure you receive all your powers and more.

Dokkaebis were quickly falling to the horde of new half-breeds that the daimyo had conjured. Jaewon and the Dragon Fighters were being pushed back, away from Kira. Taejo, Major Pak, and Kwan were trapped on the other side, as their saulabis were picked off one by one.

They've never appreciated your powers. They called you demon and monster. They tried to kill you.

A vision of the stoning she'd endured flashed before her eyes.

They've always hated you. The king wished you dead since

you were a babe. He wanted you to die. You have no one. These people are not really your friends. They feel sorry for you. And yet you bring them nothing but death.

Her eyes scanned the crowd. She saw Jaewon and Captain Ha in a desperate fight against the half-breeds. On her other side, Taejo and her brother were surrounded by dokkaebis that were slowly being destroyed. It was her worst nightmare.

Then the fires surrounding her suddenly disappeared and she felt her body floating through the air. The daimyo stood waiting for her, a smirk on his scarred face as he compelled her to him.

"Look at what you have done, my child," he said with an expansive gesture of his arms. "You have brought me the Musado."

He displayed the tidal stone and jeweled dagger in his hands.

"And now you will wield these treasures and end this war," he said. "You will bring us the jade belt and then we will take over the world."

Inside her head, Kira desperately tried to undo his absolute control. The pressure of having another being in her mind was painful. The blood vessels in her nose ruptured and began to bleed. She felt a tear fall from her eye. One tear. But then, she realized that it was a tear of her own making.

"I will kill your pathetic lover first and save the prince and your brothers for last," he said. The imoogi let out a pained shriek. The daimyo turned to it, distracted. The Iron Army had drawn black blood from the monster.

The daimyo gasped. "My lord!" he shouted. "I will be there soon."

Then Kira blinked her eyes. He didn't even notice. She blinked them again and moved her fingers. His control was not so absolute after all. It was strange that when she was under the daimyo's power, she didn't hear the Demon Lord at all. But if the Demon Lord only existed in their world through the daimyo's efforts, then the daimyo's power over her could not be absolute. Kira knew she had to break free. She redoubled her efforts to regain control.

"Such a pity about your tiger spirit," he said. "It died protecting you. Like everyone else in your life."

Blinding fury coursed through her and for a brief moment, she felt the vise breaking apart.

"You made a good effort, but it was not enough. How sad is that? Pathetic really. All this effort only to fail. But that is your life, isn't it? No one has ever liked you. Even your father was ashamed of you."

At those words, Kira's fist clenched tight and her eyes locked in on those of the daimyo before her. This time her mind pushed hard against the daimyo's control and forced him from her head. The foreign intrusion was gone. With all her might, she sent a crushing blow into her enemy's face, knocking him flat on the ground.

"That was your mistake!" Kira was shaking with fury.

"My father loved me and believed in me! And I will never let him down!"

The daimyo lunged at her with the jeweled dagger. Kira grabbed his arm and twisted it fiercely. She smashed her elbow into it, snapping the bone. He screamed and dropped the dagger, falling down with an expression of shocked pain. Kira kneed him in the face several times, causing him to drop the tidal stone also. She snatched up the dagger and the fallen stone just as she was hit with a shock of burning energy. Lightning was streaking from the daimyo's fingertips straight toward Kira. She could smell the smoke rising from her uniform. Though her hair began to singe, she suddenly realized that the lightning was not hurting her. It had even stopped her nose from bleeding. She wiped the blood from her face with a dirty sleeve, and wondered what it was that protected her. On her chest, she felt an unusual coldness. Placing her hand over it, she found that the dragon of the east had frozen solid. It was he who was protecting her from harm.

Now she could destroy the daimyo.

But before she could make her move, Jaewon rushed forward with his sword drawn, trying to protect her. The daimyo saw the danger, and turned in his direction. With a flick of his fingers, he sent Jaewon flying through the air, smashing against a boulder, Jaewon's own sword impaling him through his abdomen.

"No!" Kira screamed.

The daimyo turned to her in stunned amazement.

"How is this possible? How are you still alive?"

The jeweled dagger trembled in her hands. Tears trembled in her eyes as she stared at the surprise and pain in Jaewon's face. With a hoarse yell, she stabbed the dagger into the ground and opened up a chasm that sucked in all the half-breeds and demons. The daimyo struck her again with a lightning bolt. Kira looked at him with fierce eyes. She twisted the dagger and closed the chasm. Now Taejo and Kwan and what was left of the Dragon Fighters, dokkaebis, and the saulabis rushed to her aid.

A lightning bolt flew streaking out of the daimyo's fingertips, taking out several dokkaebis and sending pieces of their inanimate essence burning to the ground.

"Stay back," Kira warned them. "Someone please help Jaewon."

The daimyo raised another lightning strike against Kira. Even as it heated up the air all around her, she continued to move toward him, unaffected. He began to retreat, his face twisted in shocked amazement.

Cursing, the daimyo began to chant in demon tongues. Taejo froze and rose into the air. Gom squealed and jumped onto Taejo's leg, while Major Pak wrapped his arms around the prince's waist, trying to pull him down.

The earth began to tremble under their feet again. They heard the imoogi slithering toward them, trying to join its minion.

In that instant, Kira threw the jeweled dagger into the daimyo's open mouth. Her aim was true; the dagger cleaved his throat.

Still alive and choking on blood, he raised a shaking finger to strike Taejo with lightning, but Kira blocked his way.

"I don't think so," she said. She pulled the jeweled dagger from his mouth and gutted him with it. But in her mind, all she could see was Jaewon's sword stabbing him. She turned back to see Seung and several soldiers carrying Jaewon's body to safety. She started to go to him when the imoogi let out an unearthly shriek in response and started to flail.

"Now, Kira!" Nara yelled. "Now is the time to finish him!"

Kira tore her gaze from her injured friend and she started running toward the imoogi, but still she was not close enough. She desperately wished for her tiger spirit. Her soul seemed to ache with the loss of what she realized was her first true friend. She knew she would give anything to have her tiger spirit back.

And then, there was a chorus of roars. The roars filled the air as hundreds of tigers came rushing down from the mountains and forests. Five hundred, and then seven hundred, and then over a thousand.

She could not believe her eyes. Even those battling paused midfight to gawk at the vision before them.

A large white tiger came bounding toward her, similar to her own spirit, and appeared at her side. Without hesitating, Kira jumped on its back and urged it toward the imoogi. All the tigers began attacking it, along with the men of the Third and Fourth Divisions. Then the imoogi lowered its head and tried to swallow Kira. She sliced at its mouth, taking out the front fang. She leaped into the air and climbed on top of the imoogi's head, holding on tight as it tried to shake her loose. With one powerful, fluid movement she rammed the jeweled dagger straight down through its head. The imoogi fell to the ground and the tigers converged on it. And then, Kira pulled out her sword and with one powerful swing, chopped off the great imoogi's head.

At that moment, all the possessed demon soldiers fell to the ground, leaving piles of skin. The Yamato and Kudara soldiers who'd fought for the daimyo immediately threw down their weapons in surrender. They cried out for mercy, explaining that they fought out of fear of being turned into demons.

A tumultuous cheering erupted from the army. Chants for the Demon Slayer filled the air. But Kira didn't hear any of it. She moved like someone old and beaten down by life. The soldiers didn't dare come too close to her, as the tigers flanked her. She didn't hear the calls of her brother or Taejo, nor was she aware of Taejo as he climbed up onto the coils of the dead imoogi and declared himself king.

"Bow down before your king! The king of the united kingdoms!" His proclamation was repeated over and over as waves of soldiers knelt before Taejo.

But Kira heard nothing. She didn't hear as the tigers roared one final time and disappeared back into the mountains. She didn't hear the cheers of all the soldiers shouting her name.

It was all just noise to her as she stumbled back to Jaewon. In her mind's eye, she could see him being impaled by his sword. She bit back the scream that was building in her throat. Seung was crying by Jaewon's side. The sword had been removed and his abdomen tightly bandaged, but Kira realized it was too late.

She knelt down and held his hand. Nara had been right. She should have told him how she felt. She should have let him know that his feelings weren't one-sided. That she would have gladly spent the rest of her life with him. She was filled with regret and a pain so wrenching that she knew her heart was breaking. And yet she had no tears. She was too broken. Exhausted, she placed her head on his chest and closed her eyes, listening to the slowly weakening beat of his heart.

"Mother, Father," she whispered. "What am I to do? How can I lose him, too? I love him."

A voice was calling to her. She recognized it as the Heavenly Maiden Lady Mina speaking directly into her mind.

"If you could choose between having your tiger spirit again or having your greatest love, how would you choose? Answer with your heart, and your wish will be granted."

The choice was easy. Her heart whispered an answer.

The next moment, she found herself in a waking vision. No longer was she on a battlefield, surrounded by the dead and injured. Now she was walking on a mountain path that she recognized as the road back to the Diamond Mountains. It was a beautiful summer day and the clear water creek rushed past in full capacity. Up ahead she made out the outline of the beautiful golden bridge that led to the Nine Dragons Waterfall. She spotted someone on the path ahead of her. She would know that tall, lean form anywhere. Her heart beating fiercely, she chased after him.

Before she could call his name, Jaewon let out a cry of delight and ran for the bridge. On the other side was a young boy, jumping and waving his arms, an expression of great happiness and excitement on his young face.

"*Hyun!* Hyun!" the young boy shouted, calling him older brother. "You're finally here! I've been waiting for you for so long!"

Jaewon had reached the bridge and was now turned sideways. Kira saw his expression of disbelief turn to happiness.

"Jaeho! Is that really you? I've missed you so much!"

Something told her that if Jaewon reached the other side, it would be too late. Running, she shouted at the top of her voice. "Kim Jaewon! Wait! Please don't go! Please don't leave me!"

Jaewon stopped halfway over the bridge and turned his head, startled to see her there.

"Kira, what are you doing here?" he asked.

"You have to stop, please don't cross that bridge," she begged.

"No, Hyun! Don't listen to that bad girl!" Jaeho demanded from the other side. "You must come to me! I've been waiting for you for so long. Please, Hyun!"

Jaewon looked torn between his two desires—one to be with his brother again and the other to be with his true love.

Kira ran as close as she could to the bridge but did not touch it. There was a shimmer in the air between her and the bridge. She was not allowed to pass. On the other side, Jaeho was also stuck, unable to reach his older brother and begging for him to cross. After a moment of indecision, Jaewon turned around to face her, concern etched on his face.

"Kang Kira, you shouldn't be here," he said. "Don't you need to be by the prince's side?"

"He is fine," Kira said, trying to keep her tears from falling. "Because of you, he is alive and will be king."

Jaewon's expression softened. "That is wonderful news. I'm so happy for you both." He shifted his body as he heard his brother's entreaties to come to him.

"I'm so glad you came," he said. "It is good to see you one last time."

He turned to continue over the bridge but Kira slammed her hand on the bridge and cried out in pain.

Alarmed, Jaewon started to head back to her. "Are you all right? Please don't touch the bridge! You cannot cross here, it isn't safe for you."

Kira shook her head. "I don't want you to leave me."

He froze, uncertain. He took several more steps

toward her, ignoring the pleas of his brother.

"It's too late," he said. "I can't be in your world anymore. I must move on."

"No! I don't believe it! I don't believe you're supposed to leave me!" Kira was crying. "I wouldn't be here. I couldn't be here. They told me I had a choice and I chose you. Now you must choose! You can choose to come back to me."

Jaewon shook his head. "How can I? I'm already dead."

Suddenly, a golden rope appeared and a figure floated down from the heavens. Kira was not surprised to see Lady Mina smiling at her from the other side of the bridge.

"Kim Jaewon, you do have a choice," she said. "You can join your brother in heaven or you may return to the living world with Kang Kira. It is up to you."

Jaeho whimpered at her side. "I want my big brother," he cried.

Jaewon stood still, his expression torn with longing for two different people.

"He needs me," Jaewon said. "And I owe him my life."

With a reluctant glance back at Kira, he headed toward his brother.

"No, don't! Jaewon! I need you more!" Kira shouted. She turned her attention to Jaeho and dropped to her knees.

"Please, Jaeho, please let him come back to me," Kira pleaded. "I know you miss him, but I need him too. He's my best friend. I don't know how I can go on without him in my life bothering me and teasing me."

At her words, Jaewon stopped and faced her with hope brightening his face.

"I thought you hated my teasing," he said.

"I don't hate it, I've never hated it. It made me feel like a normal person. You're my friend. You've never made me feel like I was a monster that didn't belong here. I might get mad at you, but it never lasts, because I love you," she said.

Jaewon turned to fully face her, and slowly began to walk toward her end of the bridge.

"You said they gave you a choice," he said. "What was it?"

Kira wiped at her tears. "I had to choose between having my tiger spirit again or having you," she replied.

A broad smile covered his face and then he ran to her. They embraced as only two people nearly parted forever could embrace. They were both crying so hard that she couldn't tell whose tears it was that covered her face. He kissed her with all the love in his heart and she returned it in full measure. This was right. He was the right choice.

"Hyun!" Jaeho's disappointed voice reached them.

"Jaeho, I'll see you again, little brother," Jaewon said. "I promise."

"And I will take good care of him," she said.

"You mean I'll take good care of you," he retorted.

As they turned away from the bridge, Kira caught

sight of a familiar face standing behind Jaeho and Lady Mina. It was her uncle Eojin, handsome again and smiling at her. She stopped in shock. Her uncle was finally free. She'd kept her promise. Kira bowed deeply. He inclined his head and raised one fist to his chest in gratitude. And then all three disappeared from her view.

Kira awoke with a start; she heard Seung blubbering with relief and happiness. He was raving about a miracle. She lifted her head and looked down at Jaewon's smiling face.

"I had this amazing dream," he said. "I dreamed that you chose me and said you loved me."

She kissed him.

"I don't approve of this behavior at all!" she heard Kwan griping from behind them. "I'm going to have to hurt that boy."

"Don't you dare," Taejo replied. "I order you to leave them alone."

Kira laughed softly against her beloved's lips.

"I knew he was going to make a great king," Jaewon whispered.

"Stop talking," Kira commanded. And kissed him again.

Epilogue

The day of Taejo's coronation was also his thirteenth birthday, the fifth month and twenty-ninth day of the solar calendar. They'd returned to Hansong, which had now been named the new capital of Coryo, the united Seven Kingdoms. There was much to rebuild.

Taejo offered Kira a position on the High Council, but she refused. Instead, she accepted a special title as King's Adviser. The High Council was made up of General Rah, the former ambassador from Oakcho who had proven himself to be a great diplomat, a wise adviser, and a fine military leader; General Nam, the Guru minister of military affairs who was pivotal in the strategic planning of the various armies; and Lord Hwang, the Guru minister of foreign affairs who had helped Kira and Taejo escape from Hansong. The three men were raised to the highest position of nobility.

To Kira's great delight, her oldest brother Kyoung was made Supreme Commander and minister of military affairs. He was the highest ranking general in all of the united kingdoms. And both Kwan and Major Pak were made commanding officers of their own armies. She knew her parents would have been so proud of their sons.

Brother Woojin would stay on as Taejo's spiritual adviser. But when asked what positions Jaewon and Seung would like, everyone was surprised to hear their answer.

"Thank you kindly, Your Majesty. But Seung would like to go home to his family and eventually, I too will have a responsibility to lead my clan, when my father retires. Now that the peninsula is safe, they will return to Wagay Village in Kaya. In the meantime, I'd like to travel around some more, preferably revisit Modo and Jindo Islands," Jaewon said, glancing slyly at Kira.

"I think I might have to go with you," Kira replied. "There's a little girl who is waiting for me to keep a promise."

"You know, Admiral Yi told me that the miraculous bridge is set to appear again next month," he said.

Kira smiled at him. "I hear it is a beautiful sight not to be missed."

Taejo looked back and forth at the two of them with a puzzled expression.

"I don't get it," Taejo said. "Didn't you both run across

that once already and nearly get drowned? Why would you ever want to go back?"

Kira and Jaewon looked at each other and smiled.

The coronation was held on a beautiful summer day. Master Roshi of the Dragon Springs Temple arrived with several hundred of his brothers all clothed in bright orange and gray robes. In a private ceremony witnessed only by family, the High Council, and his close friends, Taejo was crowned King of Coryo by Master Roshi.

After the private ceremony, the new king was carried by an elaborate black-lacquered palanquin to the palace courtyard, where all the nobles and royals in their best hanboks were lined up to bear witness to the coronation proclamation. The three members of the High Council stood by the golden dragon throne. Kira and her brothers stood behind the throne while Brother Woojin, Seung, and Jaewon stood off to the side. Not far away, Nara had a place as an honored guest. She was dressed in a purple silk hanbok and adorned with so much jewelry that everyone wondered who the mysterious visiting princess could be. Jindo and Gom kept her close company, sitting at her feet and keeping the curious away.

Lord Rah read the official coronation notice.

"'It is hereby established that the once separate kingdoms of Hansong, Guru, Tongey, Oakcho, Jinhan, Kaya, and Kudara are now united into one nation. The united kingdom of Coryo. All will swear fealty to the new king of Coryo."

As Taejo walked the length of the courtyard, Lord Rah stepped forward. "All hail Coryo, the united Seven Kingdoms! *Manse!*"

"Manse!" answered the crowd.

Kira felt a rush of pride. *Manse,* ten thousand years. There was no greater honor.

Next, Lord Nam addressed the crowd. "All hail the new King of Coryo! *Manse!*"

"Manse!"

Taejo was almost near the dais when Lord Hwang raised his arms to the skies. "All hail King Taejo! *Manse!*"

"Manse!"

Taejo stepped onto the dais and stood in front of the throne. Shouts of *"manse"* continued as the nobles threw up their hands with each cry. Then a sudden darkness fell over the crowd. Something was blocking the sun. People started pointing in the air and screaming. A large, bright creature was fast approaching. A beautiful silver dragon landed in the middle of the courtyard. As the nobles scrambled away in fright, it quickly transformed into an old man, with long white hair and a matching beard. It was the old Dragon King, King Dang.

"Greetings to the heir of my throne and the new king of a new country. You have once again reunited the Seven Kingdoms. My prophecy has been fulfilled and I can take back my treasures," he said.

At his words, Kira hastened to his side and handed over the tidal stone, jeweled dagger, and jade belt. The belt had been retrieved from its special hiding place in Flower

Hill Temple before she'd returned to Hansong.

As she handed over the tidal stone, however, Kira felt a pang of loss to be parted from the ruby that had become so dear to her. It was not its power that she would miss, but the connection that she'd had with it.

"Thank you, my child, for taking such good care of my treasures. May they never be needed again in this world," he said. He wrapped the belt around his waist. A shiver of energy passed through the belt and each of the dragon figurines seemed to thrum. "You always kept the treasures separate for good reason. But watch what happens when they are all combined."

He slipped the jeweled dagger into a loop within the belt and then placed the ruby in the hole that had sat empty in the belt buckle. A shimmering glow rose up from the trio of treasures and then several bursts of light came shooting from the belt, each a living replica of the dragon figures. Thirteen dragons circled the air above them. Kira recognized each dragon by comparing it to the figurines she'd memorized. The only one missing was the silver dragon of the east. The one that had always reminded her of King Dang.

They were a magnificent sight. An auspicious omen for the coronation of a new king. The dragons soared through the air, a dance by the most powerful creatures in the world. They climbed higher and higher until they disappeared into the clouds. The stunned audience cheered so loudly, Kira was sure that the heavens could hear them.

"The fourteenth dragon, as you know, is currently on

a chain around your neck," the Dragon King said with a wink.

Kira placed a hand on her chest with a sudden start. She'd forgotten to replace the dragon of the east on the belt.

"I'm so sorry," she said, preparing to take it off.

"No, keep it," he said. "Let it be a reminder of who you are. You are the Dragon Musado. The One of the prophecy. 'Seven kingdoms became three. Three kingdoms became one.'"

He inclined his head to Taejo.

"And One saved us all."

At these last words of the prophecy, he looked directly at Kira and bowed deeply.

Then the old man stepped back into the middle of the courtyard and once again transformed into the pure silver dragon. He shot up straight into the air, like a bolt of lightning rising from the ground before disappearing from sight.

Taejo stood at the center of the dais and raised up his arms. "All hail the Dragon Musado! *Manse!*"

"Manse! Manse! Manse!"

But Kira wasn't listening.

There was a lightness in her heart that she had not felt since she was a little girl. All the burdens she'd carried were gone. All her fear and anxiety had suddenly disappeared. She stood staring into the blue sky and watched the silver light disappear. The last of her responsibilities had flown away with the Dragon King.

At long last, she was free.

Glossary

Baduk—Korean term for the ancient Chinese board game Weiqi and the Japanese game Go

Chollima—winged horses that can fly

Daegam—Your Eminence or Your Excellency; term of respect used for high-ranking officials

Daimyo—powerful Japanese feudal lord

Dokkaebi—goblinlike creatures made from inanimate objects; always carry cudgels, which is where their magic comes from

Dongji—winter solstice; usually falls on December 22 of the solar calendar

Gisaeng—female entertainers

Haetae—mythical fire-eating dog

Hanbok—traditional Korean dress

Hanja—Korean name for Chinese characters used to write the Korean language

Hyun—boy's honorific term for an older brother

Imoogi—half-dragon, half-snake mythical creature

Jangseung—totem poles made of wood or stone traditionally used to ward off evil spirits; also used as village boundary markers

Jesa—memorial service

Ki—life-force energy

Kumiho—nine-tailed fox demon

Li—Korean measurement unit; 1 li is equivalent to 500 meters, 0.5 kilometers, or 0.31 miles.

Makkoli—milky rice wine drink

Manse—ten thousand years

Musado—warrior

Nambawi—traditional winter hat

Noona—boy's honorific term for an older sister

Ondol—a floor heating system unique to Korea

Oppa—girl's honorific term for an older brother

Sang gum hyung—double-sword form

Saulabi—soldier

Suchae—untouchables, the lowest members of the caste system, including actors, butchers, hunters, and prostitutes

Sunim—honorific term used for monks

Taekkyon—the original martial art form of ancient Korea that has evolved into what is referred to as tae kwon do

Ungnyeo—name of woman who used to be a bear and was turned into a woman by the Hwanung, a son of the Heavenly Father

Ya—hey; can also mean "you"

Acknowledgments

So this is the end. *Bittersweet* is really the perfect word to describe how I feel now that the Prophecy series is finished. I'm sad to be leaving Kira and her friends behind. But I'm also really proud to have completed the story the way I had always envisioned it, so many years ago. And all along the way, I was helped by a small army of people, who I will always be grateful to.

My eternal gratitude to:

Alyson Day, who I believe is the most awesome and coolest editor in all of NYC and whose sharp editorial eye and deep empathy for the characters and story helped push me to develop a richer, more layered story. Thank you for helping me grow as a writer.

The entire HarperTeen team who worked on the Prophecy series, for always giving me the best support and always encouraging me. Special shout-out to Alana Whitman, my selfie buddy, for always answering even the dumbest of questions. And Joel Tippie and Amy Ryan for making an author's dream come true with three of the most gorgeous covers ever published.

My amazing agent, Barry Goldblatt, and Tricia Ready for knowing exactly how to soothe a neurotic writer.

Caroline Richmond, Mike Jung, and Martha White, who are always there to read the best and worst of drafts. And my writing friends, who I seriously couldn't do without—Cindy Pon, Lamar Giles, Joe Monti, Marie Lu, Elsie Chapman, Juliet Grames, Robin LaFevers, and the incredibly talented illustrator Virginia Allyn.

John and Virginia Rah for always being there for me. I'm so blessed to have you in my life. Sylvia and Stu Lara, Anna Kim, and Jennifer Um, thanks for always having my back.

My sister, Janet, and my brother-in-law, Laurent, for being the most enthusiastic supporters of my books and who own more copies of my books than even I do. You guys are the best. To Mom and Dad for always being so supportive and proud.

To Summer, Skye, and Gracie, I'm your number one fan for always. And to my husband, Sonny, you always believed in me. This is one "I told you so" that I'll let you hold over my head forever.

And to all my readers everywhere—thanks for being a part of Kira's journey.